VALERIE CONWAY couldn't believe Kim wanted to make amends for the past. She was sure this was a ploy of Kim's to [illegible] son's heart. But Va[illegible]ld never happen[illegible]'s children as p[illegible]

KIM DIXON [illegible] sister-in-law r[illegible] how she realized that she had an unscrupulous, relentless enemy in Valerie. As long as Valerie remained in Oakdale, Kim was in jeopardy.

JOHN DIXON blamed his failures in life on his former colleagues at Memorial Hospital. He started drinking again to forget the humiliating betrayal, but the pain only became more acute. With alcohol strengthening his resolve, he vowed to show them all that though he might be down, he was never out.

Series Story Editor **Mary Ann Cooper** is America's foremost soap opera expert. She writes a nationally syndicated column, is a major contributor to soap opera magazines, and has appeared on numerous radio and television talk shows.

Angelica Aimes, author of *The Second Time Around*, is a celebrated romance writer. A native New Englander, she now divides her time between her Manhattan townhouse and her cottage on a secluded island in the Atlantic.

From the editor's desk...

Dear Friend,

Captivating . . . exciting . . . heartwarming . . . these are but a few of the comments we've received from Soaps & Serials readers. We're delighted. Every month the fine team of writers and editors at Pioneer pool all their resources to bring you seven new spectacular books.

Based on actual scripts from AS THE WORLD TURNS, each novel is written with you in mind. Soaps & Serials take you back to the very beginning of the show, revealing the innocent and infamous pasts of your favorite characters, recreating cherished moments from your favorite episodes. And though each book is a complete, satisfying read, our sensational cliffhanger ending is just a hint of the drama that will unfold in next month's Soaps & Serials book.

We've recently received numerous requests for previous volumes of Soaps & Serials. If you are also curious about how it all began—or if you want to complete your collection—please see the order form inserted in this book.

For Soaps & Serials,

Rosalind Noonan

Rosalind Noonan
Editor-in-Chief

AS THE WORLD TURNS

13

The Second Time Around

PIONEER COMMUNICATIONS NETWORK, INC.

The Second Time Around

AS THE WORLD TURNS paperback novels are
published and distributed by Pioneer Communications
Network, Inc.

Copyright © MCMLXXXVII by Procter and Gamble
Productions, Inc.

All rights reserved including the right to reproduce this
book or portions thereof in any form whatsoever. For
information write to: Pioneer Communications Network,
Inc., 825 Brook Street, Box 5006, Rocky Hill, CT 06067.

SOAPS & SERIALS® is a registered trademark of Pioneer
Communications Network, Inc.

ISBN: 1-55726-002-8

Printed in Canada

10 9 8 7 6 5 4 3 2 1

Mary Ann Remembers

AS THE WORLD TURNS

During his first few months on the show, Larry Bryggman's character, Dr. John Dixon, seemed to flounder for lack of a storyline. He may have stayed forever in the shadows on AS THE WORLD TURNS had it not been for a hunch played by Irna Phillips, head writer of the show.

One day she spotted Larry and Kathryn Hays, the actress who played Kim, in the same scene. She decided that the chemistry was perfect and paired them in an on-going storyline. It was an instant success with viewers.

In book thirteen of the AS THE WORLD TURNS series, John and Kim share the intimacy of their baby's impending birth. Viewers never fully accepted them as man and wife, but the show's fans were surely captivated by their on-screen rapport. Years later Larry admitted that he and Kathryn did not "hit it off" immediately in real life, though they eventually developed a special rapport as time went on.

Chapter One
Renewed Doubts

The table was set for romance. Indigo-blue china bordered with a fine gold line lay on the palest blue linen cloth. Flanking a centerpiece of bachelor buttons and yellow marguerites, candles the same shade of blue as the cloth spiraled up from petal-shaped crystal holders; their warm honey light flickered on Sandy Garrison's flushed cheeks. A table for two. The aroma of veal Marsala spiced the air.

"This is incredible, Kevin," she exclaimed, sampling the veal. "I mean, the food and everything. It's better than an elegant restaurant. But you shouldn't have bothered just for me. It's such a waste."

"There you go again," he scolded, "putting yourself down. Which one of your husbands made you feel so insecure—Norm Garrison or Bob Hughes?"

Sandy sliced off the tender tip of a fresh

asparagus spear. It was perfectly cooked and topped with a lemony film of hollandaise sauce. But she couldn't savor the succulent taste. Kevin Thompson's acid question burned in her mind. Had her husbands left her emotionally crippled? Not Bob. She'd been proud to be his wife, even though they'd stayed together less than a year. They'd married out of need, not love, when both of them were at low points in their lives. Before the ink was dry on their marriage license they had realized their mistake. Still, Bob was the best thing that had ever happened to her; it certainly wasn't his fault that she was always putting herself down. But Norm . . . burly, overbearing Norman Garrison, a rough-edged diamond who'd wanted every woman except his wife?

It was true; Sandy couldn't deny it. Along with the white Cadillac and the fat life insurance policy, Norm had left her a legacy of insecurity. She fixed her gaze on the soft yellow flames that glimmered in the darkened room like cats' eyes.

"Marriage to Norm would have made any woman insecure. It doesn't really have anything to do with me. I'm still the same old Sandy you've always known and loved," she admitted defensively.

Kevin arched a skeptical eyebrow and considered her across the small, round table. Sandy was still a desirable woman. He couldn't imagine any man not being drawn to her warmth and vivacity, as well as her large doelike eyes and slender, statuesque figure. "Norm has been dead for months," he reminded her gently, "and you're still putting yourself down. He must have really done a number on you."

Sandy felt the knot of tension tighten in the pit of her stomach. She had lived with this painful twinge ever since her husband was pronounced dead of a massive coronary in Oakdale Memorial Hospital. She didn't want to think about Norm's death, though. The circumstances were too painful to dredge up again. Yet she couldn't deny Kevin's words. It would be a long time before she regained her confidence and self-esteem—a long time, if ever. It had been painful enough to have her husband carry on a clandestine affair. But to have him die with the other woman in his room, and then have that information broadcast openly at a public hearing, had been devastating.

"I hope you understand that I'm speaking frankly because I'm your friend," Kevin was saying. "I care about you, Sandy. And I think you're a terrific lady, no matter what you think about yourself."

Reaching across the table, Sandy squeezed his hand reassuringly. Although she longed to avoid the topic of Norman, she knew that Kevin was only trying to help.

"Friends still?" He covered her hand with

his, blocking out the ten-carat diamond ring and the platinum wedding band that she still wore.

"Friends forever." Sandy's smile dispelled the worried shadow that had darkened her face. "And speaking of friends, I want to know all about you and Susan. I've heard a lot of juicy gossip about the two of you."

Just the mention of Susan Stewart brought a broad, revealing grin to Kevin's face. For an instant he closed his eyes and pictured her as he had first seen her in the hospital—the image of professional efficiency, looking as small and slim as a teenager in her white hospital coat. "Dr. Stewart?" he'd asked tentatively, reading her nametag.

"Pleased to meet you. Mr. Thompson, isn't it?" she'd said, walking toward his bedside and extending a hand in greeting. "I'm glad to see you're awake. I would have hated my efforts to have gone to waste. You gave me quite a scare."

"You're Dr. Stewart?" Kevin had felt stupid the instant he'd blurted out the question. He'd heard from his surgeon that a Dr. Stewart had found him unconscious by the side of the road where his motorcycle had flipped over. He had assumed it was a man to whom he owed his life.

"I'm Dr. *Susan* Stewart." Her dark hair bobbed as she nodded, and her brown eyes danced with amusement. "My ex-husband and his father are also Dr. Stewarts—Drs. Dan and David Stewart. I suppose you expected one of them."

"I am surprised," he'd admitted.

"That I'm a woman?"

"That you're such a pretty woman," he'd corrected.

Kevin smiled now as he recalled the unexpected blush that had tinted Susan's sallow cheeks. He'd been her friend ever since that meeting; he was one of the few friends who had stayed with her through the dark, tormented period that had scorched her life.

"Tell me what you've heard, Sandy," he said eagerly, "and I'll tell you if it's true."

"Nothing doing." She laughed with relief, seeing how easy it was to turn the conversation away from her own problems. "I asked first, and I want every detail. First of all, are you two happy? Judging from the silly grin on your face—"

Sandy never got a chance to finish, because an eager, breathless call interrupted her. "Kevin, darling! Are you home?"

Before he could answer, Susan burst into the room, her latchkey still dangling from her finger.

"Speak of the devil—or rather, angel, in this case," Kevin corrected quickly. A welcoming smile lit his face, making it glow more brightly than the candlelight. But one look at Susan wiped away even the faintest hint of happiness.

"Well, and look what we have here. A cozy dinner just for two," she said through clenched teeth. Her dark eyes darted around the room, registering every incriminating detail: the fine china and linen, the flickering candles, the sumptuous meal and—most telling of all, in her eyes—the plunging V neck of Sandy Garrison's sweater.

Sandy rushed to explain. "It's not what you think, Susan. Believe me. You know what good friends Kevin and I are."

"I know all too well." Susan's voice sounded as if it had been soaked in vinegar. "If this were the first time I caught you two together . . . but it seems that every time I go out of town, you and Kevin conveniently bump into each other. I suppose you're going to tell me that Kevin was just sitting down to this elaborate dinner when you dropped by to return a book you borrowed weeks ago. Of course, you happened to be wearing that flashy silver lamé sweater with the neckline plunging to your navel, and—of course—Kevin asked you to stay." Her words dripped sarcasm like wax from the candles.

"I can tell you exactly what happened, if you intend to listen," Sandy snapped back, irritation sharpening her tone.

"It's okay. Let me handle it," Kevin murmured, half under his breath. Although his words were directed at Sandy, his eyes never left Susan. They looked both wounded and pleading. Even in the best of times, Susan was a difficult, troubled woman. She'd wasted precious years of her life chasing after a lost dream—a dream that she could win back her husband, one way or another.

But once Dan had walked out of her life, he never looked back. In his heart he believed with total conviction that their marriage had been a bitter mistake. And Dan was not the kind of man to make the same mistake twice. As far as he was concerned, his life with Susan had ended permanently the day he closed the door.

After drinking heavily and sinking to the blackest point of despair, Susan was finally beginning to pull herself together. She'd gone on the wagon, with Kevin's help, and started to rebuild her career. The young Susan Stewart had been as promising a physician as her husband. Now, for the first time, she was gaining the confidence to realize that early promise.

Watching her excited face change abruptly to shock and then bitter anger, and hearing the high, hysterical note in her voice as she hurled accusations at Sandy, Kevin felt his own heart sink. How could he make Susan understand? How could he convince her that appearances could be deceiving? If their places were reversed, he would probably jump to conclusions, too.

"I'm sorry, Susan—sorrier than I can ever say." His voice was soft and his eyes were deep wells of sadness. "Not because Sandy and I have done anything to regret, but because I've poisoned your mind with suspicion."

"Poisoned my mind with suspicion!" she shouted. "No, Kevin, you haven't poisoned my mind. You've opened it to the truth."

"The truth will set you free," Sandy murmured under her breath. Although she knew Kevin didn't want her to interfere, she couldn't sit there a second longer and hold her tongue —not when one of her dearest friends was being falsely accused on her account.

"That's just what you want, isn't it?" Susan shrieked. "For Kevin to be free of me. Well, you don't have to worry any longer. You're finally getting what you want." Her voice rose in a crescendo of anger and anguish. "I'm walking out of here now. Out of your lives."

For a moment, Kevin and Sandy sat motionless, as though Susan's bitterness had immobilized them. But Kevin couldn't watch her storm out of his life. When she turned on her heel, determined to leave as abruptly as she'd come, he jumped up and rushed after her.

"I can't let you go like this—not after what we've been to each other," he insisted. Catching her wrist, he spun her around into his arms. "What do I have to do to make you believe me? Sandy and I are just friends. Can't you understand that?"

"Of course I can . . . all too well." Susan answered in a voice that could have frosted glass. "You'd do anything for a friend, Kevin, wouldn't you? *Anything.* That's what I hate about you."

"You're being unreasonable, Susan," Sandy chimed in. "You're too upset now. Why don't you go home and sleep on it, and in the morning the two of you can talk like mature adults." Sandy knew she should keep out of their fight, but she couldn't control herself. "Right now, if you ask me, Susan, you're behaving like a jerk. And if you don't cool it, you're going to say and do a lot of things you'll regret."

Susan turned on her, eyes darting like angry flames. "Shut up, damn you," she cried, every frustration, every hurt, every humiliation contained in her choked voice. "Aren't you satisfied yet? You've destroyed Kevin and me. You've poisoned the one decent thing in my life. Isn't that enough for you?"

"No, Susan. You're wrong—terribly wrong," Sandy began.

But Susan was too distraught to think clearly, too distraught to listen to anyone. She'd never intended to be away from Kevin for a day, let alone the better part of a week. But when she'd approached Dan in the hospital lounge, determined to make a clean confession, the words she had rehearsed wouldn't come out of her mouth. Instead of explaining how she had erased taped telephone messages from Kim Dixon—messages that would have changed his life forever—she'd chickened out and found herself fabricating a new lie: "I have to be out of town for a few days, Dan, so I won't be able to see Emily this week. Just wanted to let you know."

Now, in retrospect, she wished she'd said anything else—even the truth about the tape. If Susan had stayed in town with Kevin, Sandy would never have had a chance. "Be quiet. For God's sake, be quiet," she cried hysterically at the other woman. Breaking free of Kevin's arms, she ran out of the room with her hands covering her ears.

The front door slammed with a dull thud, and an eerie silence fell over the house. Kevin still stood where Susan had left him, fighting the urge to break down and cry his heart out. Instead, he swallowed hard and blinked several times, holding himself under tight control. The unshed tears stung like salt in an open wound. He had invested so much of himself in Susan—so much patience and effort, so much hope and love. Now all of it had been lost over an innocent supper with a friend, an invitation extended and accepted out of loneliness.

"Come on, Kevin. It's not the end of the world. Once Susan recovers from the shock of seeing me here, I'm sure she'll come to her senses. Why don't you sit down while I make coffee? It'll do you a world of good."

Sandy's words seemed to come to him from a great distance. But when he forced himself to focus on her, she was already clearing away the supper plates. Kevin watched her walk out to the kitchen, balancing the plates in one hand and the platter of veal in the other. Then he sat down to wait as obediently as a child.

Had he unconsciously been playing with fire when he'd invited Sandy to share an intimate supper? Under the guise of friendship, did he secretly desire something more with her, as Susan believed?

Kevin was still tormenting himself with doubts, questioning his own deepest motives when Sandy returned with coffee and the chocolate chestnut mousse he'd picked up for dessert. All through supper Kevin had been looking forward to it. Now, with the rich concoction in front of him, he had no appetite. "You help yourself, Sandy. I don't really like mousse," he lied.

"Well, at least have a cup of coffee, then," she urged. "There's nothing like a hot drink to put your problems in perspective."

"You sound like my mother." He tried to smile and failed abysmally.

"I certainly don't *feel* like your mother. After that little scene with Susan, I feel much more like a scarlet woman. Seriously, Kevin—" she sat down opposite him and sampled the dessert

17

approvingly; diet or not, it was irresistible —"I'm sorrier than I can ever say about to-night."

"It's not your fault," he cut in curtly. "I've nobody to blame but myself. Maybe Susan's right. Maybe I do like you in a way that's got nothing to do with friendship."

"That certainly is news to me." Sandy tried to brush aside his concern, but she couldn't help feeling ill at ease.

"Then you don't feel anything deeper for me?" Kevin pressed. "You're not secretly glad that Susan has left me?"

Sandy shook her head, more from the help-lessness of the situation than in answer to Kevin's question. It was obvious to her what he was doing. He was trying to justify Susan's loss. Could she make him see that, without inflict-ing an even deeper wound? Whatever the consequences, Sandy knew she had to try.

Fortifying herself with a gulp of coffee, she gazed at him sympathetically. "First of all, Kevin," she began, "I don't believe that Susan *has* left . . . at least not permanently. She just needs time to lick her wounds and learn to accept you the way you are, flaws and foibles and friends and all, not the ideal way she would like you to be. Second, your friendship is very precious to me. I'm not at all sure that I could have a deeper, more lasting feeling for you if our relationship were more . . . more intimate. Maybe if we'd met in another period of our lives, in a totally different set of circumstances, our affection would have grown in a different direction. I know some people say that a man and a woman can't be just friends. That's the way Norm felt. But I don't believe it.

"You're one of the best friends I have. I don't want anything to change that, Kevin. Besides—" Sandy smiled at him almost shyly —"there's somebody else in my life now. At least I hope there will be soon." She took a sip of coffee, moistening her lips self-consciously.

Why am I admitting this now, before anything has even happened? she asked herself as the words were spilling out of her mouth. "I haven't confessed this to anybody else, and you have to swear not to breathe a word of it to a soul . . . not even to Susan. But I'm hoping and praying that Bob will come back into my life."

"Are you serious?" Kevin stared at her in surprise. He'd heard that Bob Hughes and Valerie Conway were seeing an awful lot of each other—at least when Valerie wasn't out with Dan Stewart. "Are you seeing Bob again?"

"Not exactly," Sandy admitted. "At least not yet. I suppose you know that Bob's been dating Valerie. But he's also been coming into the Wade Bookstore whenever I'm working there. Right now we're just talking, about old times and books and all. But I can't help hoping—"

"You mean you're still in love with Bob after all these years?" Kevin was so curious that for a few moments he forgot about his own problems.

Sandy's cheeks flamed with embarrassment at Kevin's blunt question. The truth was she'd been too immature and too confused when she'd married Bob the first time. Now, looking back on her life, she realized that he'd been the best part of it. And in spite of the years that had passed, Bob was still the same kind, decent, generous man he'd always been. Only now, since the death of his wife Jennifer, he was lonely, too. "I don't honestly know what's been going on in my mind," she admitted. "But you know the old song that goes 'Love is better the second time around'? I believe that, I really do."

Kevin's face blanched as if he'd just seen a ghost. Suddenly, Sandy's concerns faded to the back of his mind as a new fear struck him. The last time he'd picked Susan up at the hospital, he'd found her talking in the lounge with her ex-husband. And the moment she got outside to the car, she'd announced that she was going out of town for a few days. Just a coincidence, or something more? he wondered. Dan Stewart was handsome, successful, and dynamic. Kevin couldn't begin to compete with him for Susan . . . or any other woman.

Doubts and fears whirled in his brain with tornado force. *Love is better the second time around*. The old song lyric rang in his head like a nightmare. If it was true for Sandy, it could be true for Susan, too. Was she truly angry and hurt? Or had she used his innocent supper with Sandy as a ready-made excuse to leave him and go back to her first husband, her first love?

Chapter Two
Unsettling Old Scores

Twenty to four. Kim Dixon consulted her watch again, as she had every five minutes for the past half hour. Her former sister-in-law had promised to meet her for a drink at three o'clock. *Forty minutes ago,* Kim thought, *but that's typical.* For years, Valerie Conway had seized every chance she got to frustrate and hurt Kim, to even an old score, as Valerie would say. But Kim knew that wasn't true.

Twirling her crystal goblet of Chablis between her fingers, Kim tried not to let Valerie's tactics upset her. After so many years, she knew she should be used to her sister-in-law's vengeful ways, but she never would be. Petty, malicious, spiteful behavior was as incomprehensible to Kim as the theory of relativity. Still, Valerie had been trying to strike back at her for years—long before Kim had moved to

Oakdale, married John Dixon, or fallen in love with Dan Stewart.

The two women went back a long way. The tension and bitterness between them went back almost as far. *So much water under the bridge,* Kim thought with a heavy sigh. *If only Valerie could see it that way, too.* Now that Valerie had moved to Oakdale, Kim was prepared to bury the hatchet, if only for Betsy Stewart's sake. She and her half sister Emily were like daughters to Kim. There was nothing she wouldn't do to help them—nothing.

The chilled wine slid smoothly down her throat, but even that didn't help her relax. Until her ordeal with Valerie was over, nothing could. Kim wished there was some way to avoid the meeting, but Betsy had asked her to help. Sipping the Chablis, Kim looked back on the bitter twists of fate that had separated her from Dan. She couldn't imagine ever loving another man as totally, as passionately, as hopelessly as she had loved Dan Stewart. And, ironically, she still loved him. If only she'd accepted his proposal when he'd begged her to marry him.

In retrospect, Kim knew it was the biggest mistake of her life. But at the time she'd been afraid of hurting Susan, of driving her even more deeply into alcoholism. Instead of accepting with all her heart, as she'd yearned to do, Kim had gone away to think over her life.

A freak accident had left her with amnesia, and by the time she regained her memory, Dan was lost to her. Desperate to recapture his love and unable to see him, she'd poured out her heart, recording her deepest, most intimate feelings on his answering machine.

Dan had never returned the call. Instead, he'd taken his two girls and flown to South America for an indefinite stay . . . without so much as a word of farewell to Kim. Now he was back in Oakdale, and she was pregnant with John's baby—not with Dan's as she secretly pretended—and he was dating Valerie.

At first, Betsy had resented Valerie, feeling that she was trying to take Kim's place in their home. Between themselves, Betsy and Emily still prayed that their fondest dream would come true. In the perfect world of their imagination, Dan and Kim would walk down the aisle together and live happily ever after with them.

It was difficult for Kim to explain why their wish was impossible, because it was the same wish she still held firmly in her heart. But she had tried to make them understand that it was Dan's choice—and right now he seemed to be choosing Valerie. Reluctantly, Betsy had asked Kim to apologize to Valerie for her. She knew that her rude, bitter behavior had strained their family ties. And she couldn't bear to think that she might have hurt her father.

"What time did you say, Kim, three or four?" Valerie's crisp, breathy voice cut through Kim's thoughts, and she looked up with a start.

"Hello, Valerie." She forced a smile. "It was three o'clock."

"I honestly couldn't remember, so I took a chance that it was four, and here I am. I suppose you're sore as hell. But, then, that's nothing new." Sliding into the blue leather banquette opposite Kim, she slipped out of her extravagant blue fox coat and signaled for the waiter. "A sherry on the rocks with a twist and another . . . whatever . . . for my friend." She waved a bejeweled hand imperiously, dismissing the waiter as quickly as she had summoned him.

Gripping her wineglass more tightly, as if that would help her keep a hold on herself, Kim observed Valerie. Her hair was perfect, as if she'd just stepped out of the beauty parlor. Her makeup, as usual, was flawless. Her tawny sweater and matching skirt were of the softest Scottish cashmere. Heavy sterling silver disks pierced her ears and twin sterling bracelets cuffed her wrist. Even a prejudiced observer would have to admit that Valerie Conway was as stylish and sophisticated as a model.

"You look terrific, Valerie," Kim said admiringly. "But you always do, of course."

"I give it the old college try." Valerie

laughed without humor and considered Kim critically. "And you . . . you look *large*, Kim. Are you sure you're not overdue?"

Instinctively Kim folded her hands protectively over her abdomen. It was true. In the last trimester of her pregnancy, she had put on a lot of weight. Still, she didn't appreciate her sister-in-law's sarcasm. The way Kim looked was perfectly natural for an expectant woman; there was no need for Valerie to rub it in.

Ignoring Valerie's question, she forced herself to keep her tone light. "I didn't ask you to meet me today to talk about myself."

"Why did you invite me?" Valerie paused while the waiter served their drinks. "I know you weren't dying for my company."

Kim's voice was hesitant at first. "That's not entirely true. I sincerely wish that we could be friends, that you would bury the hatchet. Holding a grudge for so many years must be twisting you up inside. But you're right, Valerie, that's not why I've been waiting for you. Actually, I want to talk to you about Betsy."

"Betsy!" Valerie's voice echoed her surprise. "Why have you been talking to her?"

Although she knew she shouldn't have any more wine in her condition, Kim cheated and took a sip, hoping the drink would quiet the anger that flared inside her at Valerie's sharp question. "As a matter of fact, I make a point of talking to her at least once a week. She knows she can call me anytime she feels like talking. Both Betsy and Emily are very special to me. They always will be, no matter what Dan decides to do with his life."

"You don't have to carry on with that sanctimonious hogwash in front of me." Valerie's words crackled with anger. "I know you too well to fall for it. There's only one reason you're still paying attention to those kids: you think you can control Dan through them. But this time I'm not going to let you interfere in my life. You had your chance with Dan, and you blew it. He's shut you out of his life forever and opened his heart to me."

Kim counted slowly to ten under her breath before she trusted herself to answer. "Aren't you even curious to hear what Betsy had to say?" she challenged. "She was talking about you, after all."

"The kid hates me," Valerie shot back. "Thanks to you, for poisoning her mind against me."

"That's not true," Kim insisted. "Betsy wants you to like her. It's true she resented you at first, but that's only natural for a child. Now that she understands how much you mean to Dan, she wants you to forgive her. She's sorry she tried to come between the two of you, and she's hoping you'll still be her friend. Please, Valerie, give the girl a chance. Betsy's been through so much in her short life. For a girl her age, she's suffered so many losses. You can't blame her for trying to cling to a mother image." Kim's heart was racing when she finished speaking. It was probably the most difficult speech she'd ever made in her life —begging another woman to take the place she still cherished as her own—and she hoped she'd delivered it convincingly.

"And I suppose you see yourself as that mother image." Valerie's scathing retort shattered Kim's hope. "Do you think I'm so naive that I can't see through your little ploy? You want Dan back," she accused bitterly, "and you'll stoop to anything to get him. Even using a child like Betsy."

Even as Valerie hurled her furious charges, Kim was shaking her head in total denial. "Please believe me," she pleaded. "I'm only telling you this as a favor to Betsy. She was afraid to go to you because she thinks you hate her now."

Valerie's cold, brittle laugh mocked every word Kim had said. She didn't believe for a second that Kim was sincere, any more than she believed Kim had the child's best interests at heart. Valerie judged everyone else's motives according to her own, and there was no way she would ever lift a finger to help patch up Kim and Dan's relationship. There was only one person in the world Valerie loved enough to put herself out for, and that was Valerie Conway.

"You know what I believe, Kim? I think you'll stop at nothing to get Dan back. It eats your heart out to see me—of all the available women in the world—snagging your Dr. Stewart. And you're so desperate to break us up that you'll even use an innocent child for your unscrupulous ends."

Kim blanched at her accusations and, for a frightening moment, thought she might faint. The second glass of wine had been a definite mistake in her condition, but it was too late to do anything about it now—too late to do anything about so many more important things she wished with all her heart she could change.

"That's a lie, Valerie," she murmured in a low, strained voice. "It's true that I still love Dan; I suspect I always will. But he's made his choice painfully clear. What would I gain by trying to come between the two of you? What kind of life, what chance of happiness could I expect with a man who didn't want me? I'd feel more like a burden than a helpmate."

Her sister-in-law shook her head smugly. "You seem to have conveniently forgotten something. I know you from way, way back. You may be able to fool the people here in Oakdale, but you can't pull the wool over my eyes. You're far from the angel you like to paint yourself, and I think I'll be doing the good people of this town a community service by exposing the real Kim Dixon. I think I'll make it my special business to let Dan and Betsy and Emily know exactly what kind of hypocrite you really are. When I'm through they'll be thanking their lucky stars that you didn't become the next Mrs. Stewart."

Kim listened, speechless, to Valerie's bitter words. Her face, already pale, lost all its color, and she no longer trusted her voice to speak. For years she had known that her sister-in-law resented her, but now for the first time she realized that she had an unscrupulous, relentless enemy in Valerie Conway. As long as Valerie remained in Oakdale, Kim was no longer safe.

"I met a friend of yours the other day."

Betsy looked up from her math homework shyly. Valerie's voice always sounded cool and clearly superior. It made Betsy feel that no matter what she did or how she looked it wouldn't meet with Valerie's approval. But Kim had told her if she thought positively about her father's new friend, she would begin to feel more positive. And much as she hated talking to Valerie, even that was easier than trying to figure out the math problem before her.

"Can you guess who?" Valerie sat down at the table beside Betsy and glanced at her homework sheet. Mistrustful of everything Kim said or did, she wanted to quiz Betsy herself. "Come on," she coaxed. "Give it a try. You're the one who wants to be friends," she added pointedly.

Betsy was already shaking her head, too nervous at even the prospect of being alone in the same room with Valerie to get the hint. "Uncle Dan?" she asked, the hope sounding clearly in her small voice.

"No, it wasn't your father. He was at the hospital—and that's the last place in the world I want to go. I'm such a chicken when it comes to doctors, I'm even afraid to visit a sick friend." She laughed, trying to make Betsy relax. But the sound was forced, even to her own ears. "Come on, try again," she urged, suppressing an exasperated sigh. "I understand that she's a special friend of yours . . . someone you asked to talk to me."

Color flooded Betsy's face until she was as red as a fire truck, from the Peter Pan collar of her blouse to the roots of her hair. "You mean Kim?" Her voice was a tiny, embarrassed whisper. It had never occurred to her that Kim would tell Valerie everything.

"You did ask her to talk to me, didn't you?" Valerie's tone sharpened and she studied Betsy with cold, clear eyes that demanded the whole truth.

Betsy's tongue refused to work. All she could do was nod.

"You do want us to be friends, don't you?"

"Oh, yes," Betsy managed to stammer. "I'm sorry I've been so difficult."

"You haven't really been difficult." Valerie

31

patted her head reassuringly. "You just don't like me dating Dan, and you're not very good at pretending you do."

"Then you're not mad at me?" Betsy's scarlet face brightened.

"Not at all. As a matter of fact, I've decided not to see Dan anymore. The last thing in the world I want to do is break up a happy family."

"Do you really mean it?" the young girl blurted, too surprised and excited to hide her relief.

Valerie had to laugh at the sight of Betsy's wishful, expectant face. *The kid really does hate me. But I'll teach her—and Kim Dixon. When Dan finds out what the two of them have done . . .*

As Valerie was coldly calculating exactly how she would manipulate them all, Dan walked in.

"Well, this is a surprise." He grinned happily and leaned over to plant a lingering kiss on Valerie's upturned lips. "I didn't even know you were coming over today, Val. What have you two been talking about?"

"Nothing much," Valerie answered quickly. "I was helping Betsy with her math assignment." She gave the child a conspiratorial wink. "Here, Dan, you're probably a lot better at this than I am," she said, grabbing the paper and pushing it at him. "Anyway, I've got to get going. I'm already running way behind schedule," she added, glancing at her watch and tapping it for emphasis.

"You mean the minute I get home you leave? What's going on around here, anyway? It's enough to give a guy a complex." Dan's voice was teasing, but he was secretly pleased to find Valerie and Betsy together. For weeks the tension between the two of them had been nerve-racking. Betsy's virulent resentment had troubled Dan. But, as much as he loved them, he couldn't allow his children to govern every aspect of his life. "Where are you racing off to in such a hurry?"

"If you must know," Valerie answered, gathering up her bag and gloves, "I have a date tonight."

The broad smile froze on Dan's face. "Anyone I know?" he asked tightly.

Laughing airily, Valerie blew a kiss to each of them. "I'm not the kind of girl to kiss and tell. You should know that, darling."

"I'll give you a call tomorrow, then." Dan followed her out into the foyer. "I'll leave the hospital at six o'clock so we can have a leisurely, romantic dinner together. Then later—"

"Sorry. Tomorrow night's out of the question." She brushed him off with scarcely a glance and slipped on her coat, a royal-blue oversized melton.

"How about the night after that, then?" Dan

didn't even try to keep the testiness out of his voice. He didn't know what game Valerie was playing, but whatever it was, he didn't like it.

Turning into his arms, she surprised him by wrapping herself around his neck. The sweet scent of her perfume swept over him as her lips reached up to his. Dan's arms wrapped around her, traveling down the column of her back. Seconds later she spun out of his arms as abruptly as she'd come into them.

Valerie never bothered to look back. With a little wave of her fingers, she called over her shoulder, "Let's put it this way, Dan: don't call me, I'll call you."

Dan stood in stunned silence, watching the door open and close firmly behind her. Even after she was gone, he couldn't believe his eyes or his ears. For months after losing Kim, Dan had been sure he'd never be interested in another woman. Then Valerie breezed into his life like a wave of excitement, and he began looking forward to tomorrow again. But what had he done now? Where had he gone wrong? Dan couldn't imagine. He couldn't believe her parting words.

Over the next few days, though, he discovered that Valerie was a woman of her word. Each time he called, she was warm, exciting —and unavailable. No matter what time or what day, she always had a ready excuse. She was even too busy to meet him for breakfast. "A full calendar. What can I say, Dan?"

After three days of being put off, Dan finally yelled into the phone in exasperation, "How about dinner and dancing a year from today at eight o'clock?"

"Sounds divine, darling." Valerie laughed throatily into the receiver. "Be sure to call and confirm, though," she added archly.

Slamming the phone back in its cradle, Dan buried his face in his hands. He was furious, frustrated, and thoroughly miserable. What had he done to make Valerie close him out of her life? He'd been racking his brain every day and still he hadn't come up with an answer, not even a clue. Dan hadn't felt so lonely since Kim went away, and now . . .

It pained him even to think of her pregnant with John's baby, even though John had been her husband when it happened. Blocking out those bitter thoughts, Dan tried to concentrate on Valerie. She'd made him forget Kim . . . almost. Now she was making him pay for every moment of pleasure she'd given him.

"Uncle Dan, what's the matter?" A small, anxious voice broke through his troubled thoughts.

Uncovering his face, Dan looked up and saw Betsy framed in the doorway to the den. Her innocent round face was furrowed with concern.

"Are you all right, Uncle Dan? I mean, you're not sick or something, are you?"

"I'm okay, Betsy. Tired, that's all." Although he forced himself to smile, she could see what a strain it was. "Maybe I should go to bed early tonight. And speaking of bed, shouldn't you and Emily be asleep by now?"

Tears sprang into Betsy's eyes, and she sniffled and wiped her nose with her sleeve, although she knew it wasn't allowed. "I'm sorry. I never meant to upset you," she blurted.

Dan hurried to reassure her. "I'm not mad at you, honey, just because you stayed up a little late."

"No, you don't understand."

For once, Dan was too preoccupied with his own disappointment to give Betsy the time she needed. "It's okay, whatever it is," he soothed her mechanically. "Now go to bed like a good girl, and be sure you take Emily with you. In the morning we'll have a long talk and you can tell me all about what's bothering you."

"But, Uncle Dan—," she protested.

"Please, Betsy," he insisted, kissing the top of her fair hair. "You can tell me all about it tomorrow. Promise."

She reluctantly turned away, heartbroken sobs stifled just long enough for her to get out of earshot.

Betsy fell asleep that night counting sheep and praying for the morning to come sooner than usual. She wanted to confess her guilty secret while she still had enough courage. In the morning, though, before she even woke up for school, Dan was called to the hospital on an emergency case.

Finding him gone without a word increased Betsy's turmoil. She was so upset at breakfast, refusing to eat her scrambled eggs and looking generally miserable, that the housekeeper decided she was sick and bundled her back to bed with a thermometer under her tongue and a cup of warm milk on the bedside table.

There was nothing Betsy hated more than warm milk, especially when she wasn't sick. But she was glad to be back in bed, where she could pull the covers up around her ears and hide from the world.

"Gee, Betsy, you don't look sick to me." Emily had gulped the remains of her breakfast so she could follow the older girl up to bed. "I bet you're faking 'cause you don't want to go to school today."

"Am not," Betsy muttered through the blankets. They hid every part of her except the top of her head. It wasn't really a lie. Betsy had never felt worse in her life, even when she'd had the chicken pox in South America. The man she loved with all her heart was miserable.

Uncle Dan's life is probably ruined, she told herself. *And it's all my fault.* Valerie had abandoned Dan because of her. That was why he's so gloomy and quiet all the time. He didn't play with them anymore or look over their schoolwork. He scarcely even noticed they were in the room. Betsy groaned aloud. Pangs of guilt washed over her.

"Gosh, you really are sick." Emily stared at her sister, her dark eyes wide with worry. "I'm sorry. I'll bring you home a surprise . . . bubble gum to make you feel better," she promised. "I've still got two pennies left over from—"

"No bubble gum." Their housekeeper broke in with a stern, warning voice. "What Betsy needs is a doctor. I'm going to call your father right away."

"No," Betsy wailed again. "Please don't call Daddy, Mrs. Berger. I don't need a doctor; I need Kim."

The housekeeper swallowed the lump that rose in her throat at the child's pathetic cry. What Betsy and Emily both needed more than medicine was a mother. Kim would have been perfect—exactly what Dan and his children needed to be a complete family. Instead, Valerie had taken over. Mrs. Berger shook her head disapprovingly. *There is nothing at all honest about that woman,* she thought. *Valerie Conway spells trouble for Dr. Stewart and the girls.*

Aloud, she clucked maternally at Betsy, tucking the blankets around her. "Don't you worry about a thing, honey. Mrs. Dixon is as good medicine as anything your father could prescribe. And a lot sweeter, too. I'll give her a call as soon as I get Emily off to school."

Easing back into the mountain of pillows behind her, Betsy closed her eyes and listened to her racing heart slow to a steady, confident beat. *Kim would know what to do. She always knew best.*

Three hours later, Valerie was just emerging from a steamy bubble bath when the telephone rang. Wrapping a warm bath sheet around her moist body and twisting a turban to cover her damp hair, she padded into her bedroom to answer.

"Valerie Conway speaking." The smooth, silken voice purred into the phone.

Kim didn't even bother to say good morning. She was too upset to waste a word on pleasantries. "Are you satisfied with yourself, Valerie?" she fumed. "It's not enough for you to try to hurt me, but your little games have made Betsy sick with guilt."

"I don't know what you're talking about," Valerie replied coldly. "And I'll thank you not to call up here at dawn, hurling false accusations like hand grenades." Cradling the receiver against her shoulder, she tapped a fresh pack of cigarettes against the edge of the bedside table, then extracted one and lighted it.

"I'll tell you exactly what I'm talking about," Kim snapped back. "I'm talking about the way you're manipulating Dan and Betsy, pulling their strings with a vengeance, all because of your spiteful need to get back at me. By hurting two of the people I love most in the world, you think you can finally get even, don't you?"

Swinging her legs up, Valerie leaned back in the unmade bed and inhaled deeply, a satisfied smile curling her lips. "You know what your trouble is? You think the whole world revolves around you. Miss Perfection! I can't imagine being so conceited."

"I don't care what you think of me," Kim cut in angrily. "But I do care very much about Betsy and Dan. I'm warning you, if you don't tell him today all about the game you've been playing, then I will."

"You would do that, wouldn't you? Just for sweet little Betsy!" she mocked. "But you don't have to trouble yourself. I've already decided to invite Dan over here for supper," she lied. "A romantic dinner by candlelight. I think he'll enjoy it. What do you think?"

Kim was glad that Valerie couldn't see her at that moment. She was shaking so severely, she had to clutch the receiver in both hands to hold it steady. The picture Valerie's taunting words conjured in her mind was as vivid as Technicolor and as painful as a knife wound.

"Then after we've made love"—Valerie continued to speak, not waiting for Kim to reply —"I'll tell him what's wrong with Betsy, and how you've been using her to try to interfere with our relationship."

Reaching over triumphantly, she flicked on the remote-control button and watched the colored images form on her TV screen. "Of course, you can call Dan yourself, Kim."—she stifled a yawn of boredom—"and lie to him. Tell him you never talked to Betsy, never took me out for drinks to push me to break off the relationship. But which of us do you think he'll believe . . . you or me?"

Chapter Three
Unbearable Consequences

The cafeteria of Memorial Hospital was far from elegant: stainless-steel hot tables, huge coffee urns, white plastic dishes for take-out, thick beige utilitarian mugs and plates for those who preferred to sit in the cavernous dining area. Kim glanced from the Formica-topped tables and plastic foliage to the man sitting opposite her, polishing off the last bites of apple pie. Even in such bleak surroundings, Dr. Karl Strausfield looked distinguished, she thought, as she lingered over a dish of strawberry yogurt. With dark, wavy hair swept back from a broad forehead and silver gleaming at the temples, his intelligent eyes fixed on her with undisguised interest.

"I'm sure many men have told you this, Kim, but you've never looked better." He smiled warmly. "A beautiful woman is at her best when she's pregnant. No other joy can duplicate that inner glow that seems to surround an expectant mother like a halo."

Although she shook her head in protest, Kim couldn't deny that his words made her feel special, and she needed that boost to her ego now. Separated from her husband, pregnant, and forced to watch Valerie take her place in Dan's heart, she'd never felt more alone or more unloved. "I can't understand how anyone can think that. I feel more unattractive than I ever have in my life. I'm as big as a house and as awkward as a bulldozer. No matter what I put on, I always look like a circus tent."

"Certainly not today," he assured her. "Look around this cafeteria. I don't see a single woman here who can hold a candle to you."

Kim laughed self-consciously. "It's a good thing I don't see you too often, or I'd get a swelled head to match my stomach."

"It's not a good thing for me, Kim. In fact, I was hoping we could change that." Karl was studying her with intense, serious eyes. "I'd like you to consider having dinner with me. If you'd prefer to wait until after your baby is born, I'll understand perfectly. I don't want to push you into anything that would make you uncomfortable. But I can't imagine a more pleasurable way to spend an evening than sharing it with you."

His words were as elegant as his mannerisms, Kim thought. So different from John—or even Dan. Being pregnant and single, Kim had become lonelier than she had ever anticipated. An evening with a charming, intelligent man was a tempting proposition. "That sounds wonderful," she heard herself answering. "In fact, I can't think of anything I'd like better."

"Marvelous." He flashed a smile. "Eight o'clock, tomorrow evening?"

She was about to agree when a voice piped up behind her. "Sounds very interesting. What's going on tomorrow night?"

Swiveling around, Kim saw Pat Holland poised behind her. Her white nurse's uniform was as crisp as her words had sounded.

"Good to see you, Pat." Karl glossed over the awkward moment smoothly. "This is Mrs. Dixon. Kim—"

"You can skip the introductions, doctor," Pat interrupted. "Kim Dixon and I have known each other for years. That's why it's such a surprise to see you two together."

"Life is full of surprises, Pat." He smiled coolly. "I'd invite you to join us, but I can see from your tray that you're finished, and I'd be the last one to keep you from your duties. You're taking a late break, I presume," he added, looking pointedly at his gold watch.

"I was just leaving, doctor," Pat hastened to assure him.

However curious she was to find out exactly what was going on between him and Kim, Pat knew that she'd be cutting her own throat if she got on the wrong side of the new hospital administrator. Besides, she couldn't wait to get back to the floor and telephone John. Once he knew whom his estranged wife was seeing, maybe he wouldn't waste his life crying in his scotch for her to come back. Kim had never appreciated her husband . . . certainly not the way Pat did. She'd had her eye on Dr. Dixon ever since she came to work at Memorial. But he'd been so hypnotized by his wife, he'd been blind to every other woman.

Now, at last, Pat saw her golden opportunity. And she had no intention of letting it slip through her fingers this time.

It was almost nine P.M. before Karl switched off his brass desk lamp and folded up his reading glasses. The paperwork involved in running a hospital was staggering—a never-ending trail of forms and records. Riding the elevator down to the main lobby, he thought back to the early years when he'd had his own private practice. There was no denying that he missed the intimate patient-physician contact. Still, administration brought its share of rewards as well. And in the brief time he'd served at Memorial, he'd improved the quality of patient care substantially. *That's something to be proud of,* he assured himself.

In his mind, Karl was still reviewing his successes and failures, toting up his score at Oakdale as he started out to the parking lot. The night was heavy with the threat of rain, but he was too preoccupied to notice either the weather or the man who lurked in the shadows of the front door, waiting for him.

"Strausfield!" A loud, thick voice slurred his name. "Strausfield!" Through the darkness it resounded ominously.

At the second shout, Karl turned around, uncertainty flickering in his eyes. Evening visiting hours had ended an hour earlier. There was no one else waiting in front of the hospital, no one in the parking lot beyond. Peering into the black void of night, he tried to see where the voice was coming from. Not even a shadow moved. He started to walk toward the door, back to the safety of the hospital where he could call security, when a tall figure lurched toward him.

"Dixon! What are you doing here?" he demanded sharply. His uneasiness drained away, leaving only a cold, implacable anger. John was drunk. That was clear from the way he staggered and swayed.

"Waiting for you," John mumbled.

"A singular honor," Karl mocked, making no effort to hide his disdain. He had little sympathy for a man with John Dixon's talents who allowed himself to lose control of his life. Even if their positions were reversed, Strausfield couldn't imagine behaving the way John was.

"You're a faker, Strausfield—and a cheat,"

John screamed. "But you're not getting away with it anymore."

"I'm sure I have no idea what you're talking about, Dixon." Karl turned away. He had no intention of getting into a brawl with a drunk.

Though the sight of a skilled physician reduced to such a state was pitiful, Karl had little compassion and no regrets for firing John Dixon. He had gotten exactly what was coming to him. Through his excessive drinking, John had endangered the lives of his patients and caused heated arguments among the staff.

Karl couldn't understand how Kim had ever married him in the first place. Looking at John now, advancing unsteadily toward him with his fists raised as if he were ready for a brawl, Karl wished he could turn back the clock of time so that he, not John, met and married Kim. But now was not the time for dreaming. Dixon was growing increasingly belligerent and irrational.

"You're not going to get away with this, Strausfield. I'm on to your game."

He lunged at Karl, coming so close that the smell of alcohol filled Karl's senses, nauseating him. He could have flattened Dixon with a single, glancing blow, but he detested violence in any form, under any circumstances.

"I have witnesses who saw you with my wife today," John was shouting.

Immediately, the picture of Pat Holland's

curious face poised beside their cafeteria table leaped into Karl's mind. As a gossip, Pat had few peers. He had learned that if there was any news he wanted broadcast throughout the hospital, all he had to do was confide in her. "I had a very enjoyable coffee break with your *ex*-wife," he admitted coolly. "And I intend to see a lot more of her, if she'll let me."

At those taunting words, John lost even the slender thread of control he still possessed. Grabbing Karl by the collar, he tried to gain a stranglehold. But the amount of alcohol he'd consumed distorted his judgment.

The other doctor stepped easily out of reach. His sudden, unexpected movement made John lose what little balance he still possessed. Stumbling back, he wobbled precariously for a second, teetering back and forth as if he were trying to keep from falling off a high wire. Then his knees buckled and he thudded onto the asphalt. Down but not out, he drew himself up on his knees and lunged again in the general direction of Karl's ankles, screaming accusations like obscenities. "You wanted my wife. That's why I was fired."

Karl stood just out of reach and stared down at him with an expression as cold as ice water. "I'm sorry to disillusion you, Dixon, but your charge doesn't contain even a shred of truth. What's more, I challenge you to prove it. There was a time when you could have been running this hospital. You were respected both as a physician and as an administrator—a difficult combination of talents, as I know well. But the trouble with you, Dixon, is that you're your own worst enemy.

"You had everything going for you here at Oakdale: an excellent position, professional expertise, and last—but far from least—a wonderful, supportive wife. It's no secret that you were high on the list of rising stars. But you have so many chips on your shoulder that you destroyed your own chances.

"Other doctors who would have been happy to support you turned against you. Now I don't believe you have a single friend left on the general staff. And it's not because of anything I did to you. It's what you've done to yourself. Just look at you," Karl said scornfully. "Take a good look at the estimable Dr. John Dixon groveling on the ground in a drunken heap. You tell me who's to blame. Tell me why Kim should feel anything but contempt for you, why a woman like that shouldn't make every effort to forget a mistake like you and start a new life for herself."

The storm that had been hovering overhead like a dire omen broke while Karl was talking. A curtain of rain drenched the two angry men, but Karl ignored it until he'd finished berating his ex-colleague. Finally, thoroughly disgusted and drenched to the skin, he turned up his collar and turned his back on Dixon.

Ignoring the rain that drummed on his

alcohol-fogged head, John shouted after the retreating figure: "Wait, Strausfield. You can't talk to me like that and get away with it. Do you hear me?"

When Karl didn't even break his stride, John tried to follow him, but he was so drunk he could only raise himself to a kneeling position. Crawling after Karl on his hands and knees, wet mud splattering his haggard face, he began to weep. "I'm warning you, Strausfield, keep your hands off my wife—if you know what's good for you!"

Chapter Four
A Golden Silence

"Natalie Hughes is here to see you, Jay. She says it's too urgent to wait for an appointment."

Mary Ellison's crisp voice resounded through the intercom, filling Jay Stallings's corner office and causing him to cover his ears.

"Jay," the secretary's voice repeated, "can you hear me?"

"Loud and clear, Mary—unfortunately," he snapped back, pushing in the talk button.

Natalie was the last person in the entire world Jay wanted to see. For one moment of weakness, one lapse of his marital vows, he was going to have to pay for the rest of his life. He should have seen what she was, but at the time . . .

Jay's mind flashed back to the day he would now willingly give a million dollars to wipe out of his life permanently. His wife Carol had been away and he'd been at home when Natalie had pounded on his door. He remembered her tear-streaked face and trembling voice as she begged for his aid, helpless and beautiful . . . an irresistible combination to a rough-edged, self-made man like Jay Stallings.

He consoled her the only way he knew how—taking her into his arms, and then into his bed. At the time, surrendering to Natalie seemed inevitable. But Jay had never stopped to consider the consequences. Natalie's husband Tom was not only Jay's lawyer but, worse than that, Carol's ex-husband, as well. Jay believed that Carol and Tom were still in love with each other. When Tom intercepted a phone call between Jay and Natalie and discovered their afternoon tryst, he gave her twenty-four hours to pack up her possessions and get out of his life—permanently.

Now Jay tried to put aside the disturbing memories that hung like an invisible cloud over his marriage. He'd never confessed his mistake to Carol, and she'd never questioned him, believing in his faithfulness as much as his love. But each day a secret fear gnawed deep within him: What if Carol ever found out the truth? What if Natalie took it into her head to tell all? Jay wouldn't put it past Natalie for a second.

"Show Ms. Hughes in." His voice echoed dully through the intercom.

A moment later, Natalie swung open his

office door and marched in confidently, as if she owned the place. A butter-yellow lamb's wool skirt and matching jewel-necked sweater clung revealingly to the shapely curves of her body. Watching her advance toward him, Jay's heart skipped a beat. There was no denying the powerful attraction he had toward her.

"Long time no see, Jay." Natalie smiled, aware of the exact effect she was having on him. She leaned over the desk to kiss him.

Abruptly, he turned his face aside so that Natalie's soft pink lips landed awkwardly on the square edge of his jaw. "What the hell are you doing here?" he demanded.

Sitting down without waiting for an invitation, she crossed her slender legs and leaned back as if she were looking forward to a leisurely visit. "Since I was in town, I thought I'd look up an old friend. You're not sorry I did, are you?"

"Sorry?" he snapped. "I'm sore as hell. What if Mary Ellison tells Carol you were here?" he asked, referring to his secretary.

A cold bright glint, like sunlight reflecting on a chip of ice, gleamed in Natalie's dark eyes. "Sounds perfect to me," she said evenly. "It will save me the trouble of talking to her myself."

The color drained from Jay's face, and he stared at her incredulously. "What are you talking about, Natalie?" His voice was a hoarse, strained whisper, as if he were choking.

Although he understood exactly what she was saying, he couldn't believe she was that cold-blooded.

Shrugging a shoulder with apparent disinterest, she met his gaze boldly. "Just that your wife might be interested in hearing about one certain afternoon we spent together. What do you think, Jay?"

"Are you crazy?" he managed to utter. "Do you know what that would do to Carol? She'd never forgive me."

"Your tough luck." Natalie's brittle laugh sounded like glass shattering. "And as for Carol, I don't give a damn what she thinks. All I've ever heard from you and Tom is, 'Carol, Carol, Carol.' Well, this time it's what *I* think and what *I* want that counts—and you'd better believe it."

"What do you want?" Jay's voice sank to a whisper.

Tapping her red manicured nails on the arm of the chair, she looked at him shrewdly. Natalie preferred her men rough around the edges. Not like her ex-husband. Tom Hughes, ambitious young attorney, was a white knight. But Jay Stallings was a self-made man; he'd pulled himself up the hard way—cutting corners when he had to, twisting arms if it served his advantage, doing whatever was necessary in order to get ahead. He'd built his construction company with long hours, hard work, and a conscience put on permanent hold. Jay understood that you had to pay for everything you got . . . and the time had come for Natalie to collect.

"What do I want?" she repeated in her clear, cool voice. "I want what's coming to me, that's all."

All the things that Natalie should have coming to her ran through Jay's mind—from strangling to being run out of town. But he didn't dare antagonize her any more. "I'm not sure I understand," he began tentatively.

"Come on, Jay." The first hint of annoyance penetrated her otherwise cool facade. "You're a hard-nosed businessman. You know the score. Nothing in this life is free; you get what you pay for." She stared at him intently, daring him to deny her whatever she asked for.

Breaking away from her gaze, Jay started to get up. "It's been good seeing you, Natalie. If there's—"

"Cut the innocent routine." Her voice whipped out at him like a cat-o'-nine-tails. "You got it, Jay, and now you're going to pay for it, unless you want me to pop in on your sweet wife for an honest woman-to-woman talk."

For a fraction of the second, the threat hung between them like a time bomb. Then, defeated, Jay slumped back into his chair. He looked around the familiar office as if it no longer belonged to him. He felt, for the first time in his life, that he was no longer his own man. "Okay, Natalie," he muttered. "What do you want from me? Blood?"

"I'm not that greedy." She laughed harshly again. "You keep the blood, I'll take the money—"

"No!" he shouted before she could finish. "That's blackmail." He knew that once he began paying Natalie, she'd have him by the neck. He could never stop, and she could keep on raising the ante.

Her dark eyes bored through him. "You pay or I talk," she warned. "It's simple, Jay. You're a smart enough businessman to understand. Your money for my silence."

"I can't do it, Natalie." A whining quality crept into Jay's frightened voice. "You've got to believe me."

Shrugging, Natalie swung her bag over her shoulder and started to get up. "It's fine with me, Jay. If you want Carol to know—"

"You don't understand," he cried. "She will know. That's why I can't pay you. Carol keeps the books for me. There's no way I could hide it from her."

For the first time since she'd waltzed into his office, Natalie hesitated. She'd been so confident that she had Jay between a rock and a hard place, but now she wasn't so sure. Was he lying to her? Looking at his strained, ashen face, she didn't believe he had the courage to lie. "How do I know you're telling the truth?" she challenged.

"You can look at the books yourself—or ask Mary. "She'll tell you," he insisted.

Natalie eyed him cautiously but made no further move to leave. She'd been so sure that Jay would pay her off that she'd already begun to spend the money in her mind, and nothing was going to make her walk out of that office empty-handed. If Jay couldn't pay her himself, then he'd have to find a way to get her money, and plenty of it. The wheels of her scheming mind whirled. "If you can't pay me yourself," she warned, "then you'd better find somebody who can—and find him fast."

"How can I—" he began nervously. But Natalie was too impatient to listen.

"You can find a job for me with one of your friends," she interrupted. "It better be a job that pays a bundle, or I just might forget myself and start blabbing all over Oakdale."

"Okay, okay, I get the message loud and clear," he muttered. Groaning, he ran his hands through his hair and thought of the outstanding IOUs he could collect on. "Know anything about real estate?" he questioned sharply.

"Why?"

"I know a guy who is a real estate broker. His name is Gar Kramer. He's done a lot of work for me, and he owes me one." Jay was already flipping through his telephone file looking under K. "I'll give him a call, if you think you can handle—"

"The hotter the property the more I like him," she interrupted again. "About this Gar Kramer—"

"Let me get a hold of him first."

Natalie leaned back, prepared to wait indefinitely to get what she wanted. "Okay, but remember: I'm expensive. The more I get, the less apt I'll be to open my mouth."

As the lights of the theater came back on, Bob Hughes turned to his companion and smiled. "Would you like to stop somewhere for coffee, Valerie?" he asked, hoping the eagerness in his voice wasn't as apparent to her as it was to him.

"That sounds wonderful," she replied. "But only if I can have a slice of cheesecake to go with it," she added with a wink.

Chuckling, Bob held her fur coat for her as she slid her arms into it. It felt so good to laugh again, he thought reflectively. It seemed as if he had been doing a lot of laughing lately, and he knew it was due to Valerie Conway. True, his daughter Frannie always made him happy, even in the darkest times, but Valerie made him feel special in a way that only a beautiful, attentive woman could.

As they left the movie theater, Valerie slipped her gloved hand into his, thinking how good it was to have a friend like Bob in town. Since giving Dan the brush-off she had begun to see more and more of Bob. His good-natured attitude and sensitive disposition complemented her often outrageous behavior and cynical outlook on life.

From the corner of her eye she compared Bob's looks to Dan's. Bob was handsome, there was no denying that, but his boyish good looks and dark hair streaked with silver seemed tame compared to Dan's rugged features and wavy, thick hair. Yes, she decided, she definitely preferred Dan's appearance to Bob's.

Though she tried to convince herself that it was only Dan's looks she missed, a nagging voice in the back of her mind told her it was much more. She missed his warm laughter, his amusing stories, the confident way he carried himself, even the way he said her name. If she didn't know better, she would think she was falling in love with him.

Shaking her head as if to clear it of such a preposterous idea, she turned her attention back to Bob. "Isn't the car in the other direction?" she asked, realizing she had been too engrossed in her thoughts of Dan to notice where Bob was leading her.

"I wondered when you would notice," he replied good-naturedly. "There's a little pastry shop around the corner which should satisfy your sweet tooth."

Stopping at an old brownstone across the street from a small park, he ushered her down several steps into a small, street-level café. The atmosphere was filled with turn-of-the-century charm, and the aroma of cinnamon, fresh-brewed coffee, and warm pastries permeated the air. They selected a table near the exposed-brick wall and draped their coats over a spare wrought-iron chair. The waiter approached and they each ordered coffee and cheesecake.

"This is perfect, Bob," Valerie exclaimed, taking in her surroundings. "When did you discover this little out-of-the-way place? It's so understated from the outside that I would have never noticed it."

"Actually your sister-in-law introduced me to it," he answered.

"You mean *former* sister-in-law," she responded coolly. "Kim is no longer a relative of mine."

The waiter returned with two mugs of steaming coffee and their desserts, then departed. Bob shifted uncomfortably in his chair and cleared his throat.

"Have you always felt this way about Kim," he began slowly, "or was there ever a time—"

"I really don't want to discuss her." She methodically picked up her coffee and sipped it, signalling to Bob that the subject was closed.

Sighing, Bob concentrated on his own coffee. Though he was thrilled to be dating Valerie, he couldn't deny that there were certain mysteries about her that he found disconcerting. Not only couldn't he comprehend the irrational fury that always flashed in her eyes at the mention of Kim's name, but he didn't understand where he stood with her.

He knew Valerie wasn't dating Dan anymore, but why? Originally Bob had flattered himself that she had stopped seeing Dan so she could see him exclusively. But the more Bob dated her, the more he doubted the accuracy of that theory. Perhaps Valerie's feelings for Dan weren't as resolved as Bob would have wished them to be.

"Hello, doctor."

Valerie's richly modulated voice cut through his wandering thoughts. Her warm smile melted most of the misgivings he had been building up in his mind. "Sorry," he said. "My mind must have been drifting."

"No, I'm the one who should apologize," she corrected. "I've had a lot on my mind, and I think I transferred my somber mood on to you."

"Well, if you ever want to talk, I have a very sympathetic ear. And if you ever want a good cry," he added more softly, "I have a very comforting shoulder."

His offer was so sincere that Valerie thought she might start to cry right then. "Thanks. You're a very special friend."

Nothing more? he longed to ask. But he knew the time wasn't right. There were obstacles keeping them apart, reasons he would probably never be privy to. For now all he could do was wait and hope that time would erase some of the barriers keeping their relationship from growing romantically.

"We sure got serious, didn't we," he said. "Let's have no more melancholy thoughts. Let's only think of right now, of just you and me." Picking up his mug, he toasted, "To us."

"To us," she repeated, raising her mug to his. But even as she uttered the words, she couldn't shake the image of Dan Stewart from her mind.

Chapter Five
Affirmation of Love

Out of the corner of his eye, Jay watched his wife. Her red hair glimmered in the bright light. Her cheeks glowed like the softest petals. Although he knew he should be listening more attentively, he couldn't focus on the speaker. Carol absorbed too much of his interest.

A silence hung over the conference room where the Stallingses and a dozen other couples sat in rapt attention—except for Jay. Occasionally, as they listened to the speakers, a husband or wife would turn and smile or whisper a word. Some held hands, fingers tightly entwined. A few who'd come prepared with pen and pad scribbled notes. Although they'd been strangers when they walked into the room an hour earlier, all the couples knew each other's deepest desire. All shared the same hope: they all wanted to adopt. That was why they were attending the orientation evening for prospective parents, with a panel of experts including a pediatrician, a child psychologist, a social worker, and the director of the state adoption agency.

"The joys of being adoptive parents are as great as the joys of bringing your own baby into the world—perhaps even greater, because each one of you gathered here tonight has made the conscious decision to raise a child," the final speaker was saying. She was the agency director, a small pert woman in a fitted gray suit, graying hair fastened in a bun. "Unfortunately, not all of you here tonight will see your dream come true, for a variety of reasons. Not all of you will pass our stringent screening process. You should know that we make a comprehensive investigation of the social, personal, emotional, and financial backgrounds of all prospective parents. Those that pass face a waiting period of at least two years, because there is such a shortage of healthy infants available for adoption."

Although Carol clapped at the end of the director's speech, Jay was surprised by her lack of enthusiasm. She appeared almost as disappointed as he felt. He didn't want to shatter his wife's dream, but now that he knew what was involved he didn't see any alternative.

"Is something wrong, Carol?" he asked, standing up to help her on with her coat.

"There wasn't until that last speech by the agency director. It came as a shock, didn't it?"

"I thought it was a very informative talk," he replied cautiously. Jay wasn't ready to divulge his own fear to Carol. The very thought of a thorough screening of their affairs made his stomach turn somersaults. Jay hadn't built his construction company up from a pile of scrap lumber by following every rule in the chamber of commerce guide to better business. There were those who would go so far as to say he was dishonest and unscrupulous. He preferred "tough and shrewd." No matter what adjectives were chosen to describe his tactics, however, too many of his most lucrative deals ran the gamut from shady to speculative. An investigation was the last thing he wanted for his business, and the last thing he wanted for their personal life. What if the agency uncovered his affair with Natalie? How would he ever explain that to Carol?

"I thought it was much *too* informative," Carol said in a trembling voice. "It told me a lot more than I wanted to hear." She turned and gazed up at him.

It was then he saw the tears glistening in her eyes. "Carol, you're crying." Jay's concerned voice echoed with surprise. Slipping an arm around her, he drew her gently into a secure embrace. "Why? What upset you so much?"

She looked from him to the dais where the director stood, her aquiline profile partially obscured by the couples who clustered around her in their eagerness to learn more of the details of becoming adoptive parents. "Didn't you hear what she said?" Sobs choked Carol's voice. "She said it will be two years before we get our baby. *Two years*, Jay! I've already picked out the nursery furniture."

"That's okay, honey," he said soothingly. "I'm sure there won't be any problem returning it."

A deep sob shook Carol so powerfully that he felt her whole body tremble against him. "You're so mercenary. All you can think of is the money. That's the only thing that's important to you." Her voice, usually so warm and loving, sounded bitter with accusation.

"That's not true," Jay began defensively. "I just thought—"

"It doesn't matter. Nothing matters anymore." Carol wept fiercely, burrowing her face into his shoulder.

Jay felt the questioning eyes of the other couples focus on them. "Come on, Carol," he muttered. "Let's get out of here and go someplace where we can have a little privacy."

Although she didn't answer, she didn't protest, either, as he steered her toward the door. Ten minutes later they were settled in a secluded booth in one of his favorite downtown bistros. Frothy Irish coffees in tall glass mugs were placed on the table in front of them. Fingering the handle nervously, Jay watched his wife, hoping that she would read the love and concern in his eyes. She'd never spoken to him harshly before, let alone with any trace of bitterness or disgust, and her angry words still smarted more than he cared to admit.

Carol's tears had dried. The only remaining signs of her distress were streaks of mascara that had been smudged by her tears.

"Let's drink to our baby, and to the terrific mother you'll make." Jay raised his mug to click against hers and saw a bright sheen of tears glaze her eyes again. "Do you want to tell me what's making you so upset tonight?" he pressed gently. He'd never been able to be rough or cruel with Carol. An aura of innocence seemed to surround her, in spite of the difficulties and heartaches she'd endured. Her innocence restrained his natural aggressiveness.

"Were you listening in there tonight?"

"Of course I was. We found out everything we need to know about adopting a baby." He felt foolish saying something so obvious, but he couldn't imagine what else she wanted him to answer.

"We found out too much as far as I'm concerned." Carol's lips quivered and she bit them for a moment before trusting herself to speak again. "I thought it would take a few months to get a baby, a year at the most, but two years—" Her voice broke off in a choked sob.

"That's the only thing that's bothering you?" The relief was clearly reflected in Jay's voice.

Carol could only nod her head as she fumbled in her pocketbook for a tissue.

"Look at it this way, honey," he advised brightly. "If you became pregnant tomorrow, we'd have to wait almost a year before the baby was born. One more year isn't the end of the world."

"It is if you really want a baby," she insisted. The unspoken accusation was clear in her voice—Jay didn't want a baby as much as she did, after all—and she dabbed at her eyes with the damp tissue.

"Come on, Carol, let's see a smile." He reached across the table and lightly stroked her under the chin. "If the woman said there was a five- or ten-year waiting period, I could understand your disappointment. But one year, two years . . . they'll be over before you know it. Look how long we've been married already. And I don't know about you, but it seems like just the other day that I fell in love with you." Jay tried to tease her out of her depression, but Carol lashed back at him in angry frustration.

"I'm not so sure you really love me," she charged, her moist eyes flashing indignantly. "You're probably regretting ever marrying me."

"Hold on, honey," Jay said sharply. His face paled at her unexpected charges. Had Natalie played him for a fool? Did she accept the overpriced position with Gar Kramer only to turn around and tell all to Carol?

Bloody, murderous thoughts whirled through his mind, yet he forced himself to speak evenly. "I want to know exactly what all this crazy talk is, about not loving you. If anyone—"

Carol didn't wait for him to finish. Luckily for Jay, she interrupted before he could incriminate himself. "You don't love me, Jay. It's obvious. That's why you're glad we can't get a baby for two years."

Jay's relief was so great that he felt every negative emotion drain from him. Carol didn't even suspect a thing. For once, Natalie had kept her mouth shut. "It's not why," he insisted with a huge sigh. "Believe me, Carol, that's not even close to the reason. But you are right about one thing. I don't mind waiting a couple of years for our baby—or even more, if we have to." He reached for her hand and tucked it between both of his, admiring her smooth skin and the delicate shape of her fingers. "Being married to you has made my life so full that even if something happens and we're never able to have children, my happiness will be complete. That's how much you mean to me, how very much I love you."

Tears still misted Carol's eyes, but now they were tears of happiness that glistened on her long lashes as she looked shyly into his eyes. A blush of excitement tinged her cheeks. If only

Tom had spoken to her this way, how different their lives might have been. But there was no point in looking back at a buried past now. Despite what lay concealed deep in her heart, her present and her future were with Jay. "Do you really mean that? Have I made such a difference in your life?"

Bringing her hand up against his lips, he kissed each of her fingers in turn. "No words can express what you've done for me, or how your love has steered my life like a star," he admitted. "I have to confess that the selfish part of me is even a tiny bit glad that our baby won't be arriving too soon, because I'll have you all to myself that much longer. I don't look forward to sharing you with anyone."

"But our own baby . . ." Carol's face was wreathed in proud smiles. "You couldn't really be jealous of an infant."

"Anyone, big or small, who claims your love," he insisted. "But that doesn't mean I won't love the kid, too, especially if it's a girl, a perfect miniature of you." Taking a deep drink of the warm, frothy coffee, he relaxed. All his worries had been for nothing. Natalie's payoff was keeping her quiet, and there would be no crying infants in his life for at least two years. By then, anything could happen, he thought. Carol might even get over her desire for children. For now, though, his guilty secret was safe. Natalie was a closed chapter of his life, a chapter that Carol would never be able to read.

"Maybe you're right, Jay," she conceded. A smile still lit her eyes, but her expression was thoughtful, even grave.

Downing the remainder of his drink, Jay dropped a ten-dollar bill on the table and pulled her up. "Come on, baby, I'm taking you home. You can hold me in your arms and tell me everything after—"

"After what?" She laughed as he slipped an arm around her waist.

"After I sweep you away and prove how much I love you," he teased.

Carol felt the color deepen in her cheeks even as she felt a rush of anticipation flare up her spine. . . .

Later, as they lay cradled in each other's arms, Carol stroked Jay's face as if it were a new discovery. "You know something?" she murmured.

"I know I love you, but I didn't know how much until tonight." He smiled contentedly without opening his eyes.

"Mmmm," Carol crooned. "And I love you ditto, ditto, ditto. But I was thinking about our baby."

"Our love child."

"That *is* what we'll have," she agreed softly, "when the time comes. I've been thinking

71

about what you said. I mean, about our lives being so full that you don't mind waiting for the baby."

A pang of guilt made Jay wince inwardly. He wished he'd never had to lie to Carol, never cheated on her with Natalie. If he had it to do over . . . He thought of Natalie's beautiful, sensual body. He couldn't deny that he had desired her, that he still desired her. Would he ever be unfaithful again? Jay didn't trust himself enough to answer no. But at least he could make sure that Carol never found out the truth about him.

"You were right, my love," Carol was murmuring. "Our life together is so wonderful, I'll be patient; in time, I know all my dreams will come true. You'll make them come true, Jay. I know you will."

"Yes, darling, yes," he lied with utter conviction. "Anything you want."

Chapter Six
An Unexpected Caller

The kitchen radiated a cozy, comfortable warmth. Ruffled chintz curtains in a flowered pattern seemed to dance at the darkened windows. The linoleum was the same bright blue as the collection of ceramic milk pitchers arranged on a corner shelf. The walls sparkled as white as the confectioner's sugar that Mary Ellison was sprinkling on top of a cinnamon cake she'd just taken out of the oven fifteen minutes earlier.

From the kitchen table where he nursed his second cup of coffee, John Dixon watched her put the finishing touches on the cake, as eager as a little boy for the first warm slice. He had acquired a craving for sugar since he went on the wagon, and Mary was more than happy to satisfy it. Her son would just as soon have a cookie or a dish of ice cream as a piece of cake or pie, so she hadn't done much baking since her husband Brian died. She realized now that she'd missed it. There was something relaxing in mixing a batter—creaming the butter and sugar, sifting the flour, melting the chocolate —something delightful in the aroma of baking, and something very satisfying in making a perfect cake or pie.

"Day seven." Mary smiled over her shoulder at him, giving him the encouragement that had kept him bone-dry ever since his humiliating fight with Dr. Strausfield. Mary didn't mention the fact that it would have been "day fourteen" if John hadn't fallen off the wagon the previous week.

"The seventh day and still counting," John admitted with pride. He hadn't touched a drop of liquor since the stormy night he accosted Karl in the hospital parking lot. Although John had been so drunk that night he couldn't keep his footing, no amount of alcohol could dull the mortification he'd felt. Remembering that moment now, he felt sick with shame. Karl had dressed him down with total contempt, and the worst of it was that all of his charges were true. Drunk or sober, John would never admit that to anyone except himself.

One day, he vowed silently. One day, when he was back on his feet he'd show Strausfield that Dr. John Dixon may have been down, but he was never out.

For now, though, John was still struggling to

go one more day without reaching for the bottle and the oblivion, the antidote to pain, that it would bring. He did his best not to think about Kim, because if he allowed his mind to run back over the years of their marriage—or even worse, to look ahead and imagine her in Karl Strausfield's arms—then his thin edge of control would be in instant jeopardy.

Without Mary, always there whenever he needed support and encouragement, John knew he would never have made it. Mary Ellison, widowed and left alone, worked a forty-hour week as Jay Stallings's secretary to support her son. Still, she found time to help others. In all his years as a doctor, John had never met a more selfless, caring person. They'd started out as neighbors, become friends, and now . . .

John had high hopes for a future with Mary. He felt completely at home in her cozy kitchen with her son, Teddy, dashing in and out to retrieve a forgotten toy or beg for one more cookie. They were a ready-made family to replace the one that Kim was determined to deny him. True, Mary possessed none of Kim's exuberant charm or stunning looks. She was a plain woman who clearly had never led a glamorous life. Yet her warmth and generosity more than made up for everything else. John watched with admiration as she worked.

"I could never have made it without you, Mary," he said, admitting aloud the very thoughts that were speeding through his mind. "You know that."

"I don't know any such a thing," she assured him matter-of-factly. "I think you can do just about anything you set your mind to, John Dixon."

"I think you're right," he answered quietly. "I can do anything—with you behind me."

Cutting a generous piece of cake, she brought it over to John and sat down at the table beside him, wiping her hands on her apron. *It's amazing,* she thought to herself, *how much a man can change.*

When John had moved into the house next to hers, it seemed as if the whole town had buzzed with gossip. But Mary had been through too much herself to listen. Hit with the sudden death of her husband in a freak accident and left virtually penniless, she'd learned firsthand the anguish that life bears. Instead of presuming to judge him, Mary looked at John with compassion. Tentatively at first, then with increasing confidence, she extended a warm hand of friendship. Even in his most desperate moments, John had responded. He seemed to have only one other loyal friend, Dr. Susan Stewart—a woman who knew from experience the dark morass into which John had sunk. Susan had been there herself and come through it. Seeing Susan rebuilding her life strengthened Mary's faith that John could do it, too.

Leaning back in the kitchen chair now, Mary smiled in wonder. She'd literally watched John change before her eyes, but the transformation was so amazing, she still couldn't believe it. Although he had slipped off the wagon once, the unfortunate event seemed to strengthen his resolve to remain sober. And he *would* remain sober, if Mary had any say in the matter. By filling himself with her home baking, he could satisfy the craving for sugar his body had developed from consuming so much alcohol.

John returned her smile and took another bite of cake. Mary was his port in the emotional storm that had shipwrecked his life. Her strength fired his own until he began to believe that he could have a rewarding new life, a new career. With her to help him, to support him and encourage him, he would show Strausfield and Bob Hughes . . . and Kim. He would show them all what John Dixon could do and be again.

"It won't be long now." Mary was beaming with the joy of her daydreams. "It won't be long before you'll be able to hang out your shingle again. 'John Dixon, M.D.' Or maybe you should put 'John Dixon II, M.D.' —because you are a new man. You know you are, and that would be a continual reminder for you."

Reaching over, he took her hand and covered it between his. "If I am a new man, it's thanks to you. You've become more than a friend to me, you've become a lifeline, a helpmate in the very truest sense of the word. I finally sat down yesterday and began work on that project I've been talking about for so long."

"You mean the textbook on cardiology? You really started writing it?"

Her enthusiasm was contagious, and John was nodding happily even as she posed her excited questions. "I haven't actually begun the book yet. I'm still struggling with the chapter outline, but it's a first step."

"The first of many," she replied warmly. "You're such an intelligent man. You have so much to give."

"I have so much I'd like to give you, Mary," he declared softly, "if you'll let me."

She looked down at her hand concealed between his and gently pulled it free. "You've barely touched your cake, and I baked it special for you."

Cutting once more into the slice, he obeyed with obvious disappointment. The cake was delicious, but he'd lost his taste for it. "Then your answer is no, Mary?" His words were a flat statement of the inevitable, more than a question rife with possibilities.

For a long moment Mary didn't reply. She

was searching for just the right words, words that were not so encouraging they would give him false hope or so negative they would drive him back to the despair of alcohol.

"Please try to understand," she began tentatively. "I think you're an extraordinary man to turn your life around the way you're doing, and I value your friendship more than I can say. This kitchen would be a lonely room without your company in the evenings. But I'm not ready for a new relationship yet. Brian's death was so unexpected. One hour he was healthy and happy, waving good-bye to me, and the next . . ." She swallowed, unable to go on. "I'm still not over the shock of that. I may never be, so I can't even ask you for time. It would be too unfair to you."

"What could be more unfair than deserting me now when I need you more than ever?"

A petulant edge, which Mary didn't like, colored his voice. But she reminded herself what a troubled man John was. In such a short time he'd suffered more than one man's share of heartbreak, and she would be the last person in the world to judge whether he'd brought most of it on himself.

"That's not fair, John." Although she protested, her voice was gentle and coaxing. "You know I'll always be here to help however I can, whenever you need me—but as a friend, a true and trusted friend, I hope. Besides," she added,

"I don't think you're over Kim any more than I'm over Brian."

Later that night, when John arrived home, he switched on his answering machine. Except for an occasional call from Kim's lawyer or Susan, there weren't usually any messages for him. But this evening Pat Holland's bright, confident voice filled his den.

"John, it's Pat . . . Pat Holland. It's been so long and I've thought so much about you. I'm going to be in your new neck of the woods around nine or ten P.M." There was a pause, as if she were deciding something in her own mind, then she rushed on. "If you don't want company, you can always tell me to buzz off and I'll understand. See you tonight, then."

An ominous shudder ran through him at the sound of the familiar voice. The last time Pat had called him, he had fallen off the wagon and made a fool of himself in front of Dr. Strausfield. He listened to the message a second time, still apprehensive. Relieved at the innocence of her words, he switched off the machine and glanced at his watch. He must have spent more time at Mary's than he'd realized, because it was already after ten.

A spark of pleasure gleamed in his eyes. It would be good to see Pat. She always knew all the juicy hospital gossip and was usually eager to spread it around to as many people as she could. John missed that part of Memorial as much as he missed his practice—maybe more so. The hospital was a complete world unto itself, and for years it had been his world, the only world he knew. Without a cloud of alcohol to glaze his mind, he was suddenly aware of how much he missed it.

Twenty past ten. Pat had probably come and gone while he was with Mary. He would call her in the morning, he decided. Maybe they could have dinner or—

John hadn't even finished formulating a plan in his own mind when the doorbell rang. Pat stood on his doorstep, a smile lighting her face like a neon sign, a bottle of sparkling white wine, chilled and ready to drink, in her hand.

"I just took a chance and rang the bell." She stepped in, filling the silent, empty house with her exuberance. "It's so good to see you, John. I can't believe how long it's been."

"You look terrific, Pat." John grinned in welcome. "For a couple of minutes there, I was afraid I'd missed you." Closing the door, he led the way into the den. It was the only room in the house he actually lived in, and it had an informal, well-used feel to it.

She hurried to apologize. "I hope you weren't waiting up on my account."

"Actually, I just walked in myself not five minutes ago," he assured her.

"Out on the town now that you're a free man again?" Pat joked. "Who was the lucky gal?"

"It wasn't anything like that," John said. "I was just having a cup of coffee with a neighbor."

"Well, I've brought you something a lot more potent than coffee," she said, holding up the wine bottle for his approval. "I thought we could break it open and toast the good old days at Memorial. Honestly, John—and I'm not just saying this to make you feel good—it hasn't been the same there without you. Strausfield is running the hospital like a drill sergeant, and all the rest of the doctors are afraid to take one step out of line."

All the time she was talking, John stared fixedly at the green bottle as if he were being hypnotized by it. Although he heard Pat, nothing registered on his consciousness except the temptation she offered so irresistibly. He knew that an alcoholic was never cured, that every day was a new challenge. But John didn't believe he fit that mold. So what if he'd already fallen off the wagon once? He'd had a lot to drink that night. He would have only one glass now. He wasn't a drunk. He hadn't had a drink in a week. That was a long time, wasn't it? He'd obviously licked the problem, he decided irrationally. A glass of wine with an old friend was a harmless enough pleasure to indulge in.

"Come on, John," Pat was saying. "Let's pop this cork and drink a toast to Memorial and all the happy days we had there."

Moments later John found himself grasping a

fragile stemmed glass. The pale golden wine sparkled through the crystal as he clinked glasses with Pat and raised it to his mouth. His lips felt suddenly dry. Inhaling the intoxicating fumes, he murmured, "To the hospital . . . Memorial," and took the first sip, then another, and another—each one deeper and less quenching than the one before. All too soon his glass was empty. His hand shook as he grasped the bottle to refill it. He couldn't wait to refill it, to drink again and again. Pat's features blurred like the lines of a watercolor, dissolving and reforming like shapes seen through a kaleidoscope.

"You know what I miss most about the hospital." John's words slurred together even though he made a deliberate effort to enunciate. "I miss the dirt—the gossip you were always the first to know, Pat. I don't know how you did it." Shaking his head, he reached for the bottle again, never thinking to refill hers. Now that he'd begun, there was no way he could stop himself. "You always knew everything about everyone."

"Still do," she bragged with a proud laugh. "But you've been away so long, I don't know where to begin." She sipped the cold wine she'd been nursing. One glass was more than enough to last her all evening. "Hasn't your old friend Susan Stewart been keeping you informed?"

"Susan's no friend of mine," John snarled.

Filling up his glass again, he drained it in a single gulp.

Surprised and intrigued by his angry response, Pat leaned closer, eager to uncover the reason for his bitterness. Pat's mind raced ahead, too intent on John and Susan's relationship to notice that he was polishing off the entire bottle of wine virtually by himself. There was nothing she relished more than a juicy tidbit of news she could whisper through the hospital corridors.

"Come on, now, John," she coaxed. "I know for an absolute fact that you and Susan have been friends for years."

"Susan isn't my friend." His head was shaking back and forth in adamant denial. "I thought she was. For a long time she had me fooled. But she isn't my friend. She just pretends to be to shut me up."

"Shut you up about what?" Pat's curiosity was uncontainable. Wild horses couldn't pull her out of the house until she discovered Susan's secret.

But he was still shaking his head as if he'd forgotten Pat was still waiting breathlessly to hear his story. "I thought Susan cared about me. I thought she did it to Kim for my sake, because she knew how much I loved my wife. But Susan doesn't care at all. She just wanted to keep Dan for herself. She was jealous of Kim; that's why she did it." He shook the bottle to see if it was empty, then drained the last drops into his glass.

Pat barely noticed. "You've lost me, John," she gasped. "Backtrack a little and tell me what Susan did to Kim."

John only heard her dimly, but it didn't matter. He didn't need any urging to blame his failed life on someone else. As the bitter memories washed over him, he reached for his glass again. He needed to drink now to ease the pain that festered in his heart like an open wound.

"Damn Susan." He swore into the half-empty glass. "She did it for herself, not for me. She erased the tape. I thought Kim was mine again. The amnesia had made her forget Dan . . . forget that she'd begged me for a divorce so she could marry him. I kept her locked up in our house so I would never lose her again. But she remembered him anyway. When her memory came back she must have called him because Susan found her message on his answering machine just before Dan went away. Susan and I were both glad to see him go, to get him away from Kim. But it didn't matter. I lost her anyway. I lost my wife . . . my beautiful wife."

John's voice trailed away in an incomprehensible slur. The wine was supposed to make him forget. Instead he was remembering so vividly he couldn't bear it.

Leaning toward him, Pat strained to catch every word. But it was impossible. She couldn't believe her ears, yet she didn't doubt for a moment that John was telling the truth. No one, not even John with his singular talent for deceit, could make up such a salacious story. She itched to find out every detail so she could spread it through the hospital grapevine. Wait until Dr. Strausfield found out that Kim was still secretly in love with Dr. Dan Stewart . . . or was she?

"What did Kim say in her message to Dan? Did Susan tell you?" Pat pressed.

John's hand closed around his wineglass so tightly that she was afraid he would crush it in his palm. "A love letter!" He began to rage more to himself than to Pat. "That's what she said it was. A love letter from my wife to Dan. But Kim didn't mail it. She put it on his answering machine and Susan erased it. She never let him know. He never heard a word of it." He laughed mirthlessly.

"And now?" Pat asked breathlessly. "Does Dan know, now that he's back?"

John shook his head. "It's Susan's secret," he slurred. "Susan's secret and our secret, Pat and John and Susan, secret . . ."

Incredulous, Pat stared at him, trying to put the pieces of his jumbled story together in her mind. Kim was still in love with Dan, only he didn't know it. And Kim must have thought that Dan got her message and didn't even care enough to answer her.

At first Pat had been eager to spread the story through the hospital grapevine, but now she was having second thoughts. Dan was involved with a new woman, Valerie Conway. And Dr. Strausfield was certainly interested in Kim. And then there was Susan Stewart. What price would she pay to keep her sordid secret from spilling all over the hospital?

Pat smiled to herself. John Dixon had just given her a powerful weapon—and she had every intention of using it to serve her own best interests.

Chapter Seven

All Aglow

Striking a match, Valerie raised it to the candle wick and thought of Kim. If only she could see Dan now, lying in the king-size bed. This was even better than the candlelight dinner she had told Kim she was going to have. Valerie had not intended to call Dan; she had been merely taunting Kim. The more she thought of the idea, however, the more it appealed to her. Now he was here at her request, but instead of dining by candlelight they were going to make love by it.

Waiting in Valerie's bed, Dan, too, thought of Kim. Ever since he'd found out that she was expecting John Dixon's baby, he'd tried to erase the memories of her from his heart, but she was an impossible woman to forget. Maybe it was because he had loved her so completely. Somehow, thoughts of Kim kept intruding on the new life he was trying to forge without her. When he brought the girls back to Oakdale after his self-imposed exile in South America, Dan never expected another woman to come into his life. Then he'd met Valerie, different from Kim in so many ways. Yet he couldn't deny the powerful attraction he felt for her or the distinctly jealous twinge he had felt when he heard she had been dating Bob.

Watching her light the candles, seeing the tapers' soft glow illumine her milky-white skin, he wondered not for the first time what his life would be like if he proposed to Valerie. Could she be a mother to two demanding little girls? It was impossible to picture her in the role.

Dan couldn't deny that he was worried about Betsy and Emily. They loved Kim so much that they'd had as much trouble as he'd had adjusting to a new woman in their lives, even on a temporary basis. What would they do if he announced that Valerie was moving in with them permanently? Dan wanted their happiness much more than his own. But now wasn't the time to think about anything clearly.

Valerie had finished flooding her bedroom with soft candlelight, which flattered the smooth, supple lines of her body. But, watching her approach the bed, he suddenly thought of his long-time friend and colleague, Bob Hughes, and felt the sting of his conscience.

Bob had been so terribly lonely since his wife Jennifer's unexpected death. Could Bob be happy again with Valerie? If so, Dan wouldn't want to stand in his way.

Friendship and loyalty tugged against the pull of desire in his heart. But it was impossible to think clearly now. There would be time enough to think about Bob—and Kim—in the morning, when Valerie wasn't distracting him.

"I've missed you, Val," he murmured, his voice already thick with emotion.

"I've missed you, too." Her eyes smoked with the embers of passion as she looked at him. Knowing how deeply he had loved Kim, fearing that he loved her still, Valerie had been afraid to hope for anything more than a casual relationship with Dan. Now, though, she could no longer deny her own heart. Feeling as if she, too, could love again, she dared to dream. But she didn't want him to know how very much she cared, or how deeply she had missed him.

Then, when Dan pulled her down into his arms and covered her lips with his own, Valerie forgot such matters in the power of his kiss.

"Tell me what you missed most," Dan murmured against her hair. She felt his warm breath against her ear, driving her wild with a need that only he could answer.

"I missed all of you," she whispered from the depth of her heart. "I . . ." She started to blurt out the truth, unable to contain herself, so consuming was her need to love and be loved, but he stifled with his lips the words that were about to come, forcing her total surrender in a kiss. Thoughts and memories were wiped out by their all-consuming passions.

Later, when the candles had shortened and the holders were thick with hot wax, Valerie yearned to admit what was in her heart, but even now she didn't dare. She'd forced herself to be tough, to be independent, to present a polished, impervious facade, protecting herself from the anguish of rejection. She was still too afraid to admit her feelings, to reveal her vulnerability. What if Dan didn't really care? What if Kim still claimed his heart? Valerie was too afraid to risk discovering a painful truth.

It was almost dawn when she eased free of Dan's arms, slid out of bed, and tiptoed around the room, blowing out the stubs that remained from their candlelit night of love. For a long moment she stood beside the bed and gazed at Dan's sleeping form in the gathering light of morning. Under her breath she whispered the words that burned intensely in her heart. She whispered them again and again, wondering if somehow through his sleep they would penetrate his consciousness. Then, careful not to wake him, she slipped back into bed beside him, circling his dark curly head in the nest of her arm.

When she finally woke up, the sun was bright, casting the bare maple tree outside her window in sharp relief. The delicious aroma of freshly brewed coffee wafted through the air.

"Rise and shine!" Dan was framed in the bedroom door, a steaming cup in his hand, a bright smile lighting his face. "It's good I didn't have surgery scheduled this morning. I never would have made it."

"Then, you don't have to rush off?" She answered his smile with one of equal brilliance and sat up in bed, propping the pillows behind her head.

"I didn't have to rush off at six A.M.," he corrected with a contented smile. "But I have to go to the hospital now and make my morning rounds. It's almost ten o'clock, Val. I can't believe I slept so late."

Ten was early by Valerie's standards, but she didn't want to say that. "I can think of a good reason why you overslept," she reminded him softly.

He grinned and brought her the coffee. Leaning down to place a kiss on each eyelid, he settled down on the edge of the bed beside her.

"Would you like me to give you an even better reason not to make rounds this morning?" she asked, stretching seductively for emphasis.

"I can't imagine any *better* reasons than last night," he admitted. "But I can't stay. As it is, I'm late already."

Wordlessly putting the coffee on the bedside table, she wrapped her arms around his neck and drew him to her. The temptation to surrender was so strong that he had to wrench himself free of her grasp while he still could.

"I wish I could stay," he admitted reluctantly, "but that's one of the worst parts about being a doctor. Your life is never really your own."

"I could make you forget your Hippocratic oath," Valerie promised.

"You probably could," he agreed. "That's why I'd better get out of here before I become a totally irresponsible human being."

Reaching for her coffee again, she shrugged as if she no longer cared. She was secretly delighted to see a frown cloud his face.

"What are you going to do when I go?" Dan asked so sharply that she could clearly detect a tinge of jealousy behind his words.

"Who knows?" She shrugged a second time and gave him a very private, catlike smile. "Make a few phone calls, I guess. It's too early for me to get out of bed."

Although her answer was innocent enough, Dan read a multitude of double meanings into it. *She's going to call one of her other boyfriends . . . Bob Hughes, maybe*, he thought darkly. "Well, when am I going to see you again?"

"When would you like?" She sounded as if she'd already lost interest in him.

The anguish of so many days of rejection washed over Dan again. "There's a masquerade party Saturday night," he began tentatively, afraid that Bob might have already invited Valerie to be his date. "It's a benefit for the hospital. Maybe you've heard about it."

"No, Dan," she assured him, shaking her head. "I'm new to Oakdale, remember?"

Relief flooded over him, and he grinned like a boy with his first girl. "Terrific. In that case, Val, would you like to go with me? It's sort of an annual tradition. In addition to being a fund-raiser, it's an excuse for the doctors and nurses to let off a little steam. And usually it's a lot of fun. Everybody goes all out."

"A costume party?" Valerie looked as skeptical as she sounded.

"Complete with prizes for the most original, funniest, best, and worst getup," he explained with enthusiasm. "What do you say?"

"It sounds like fun," she agreed. "What are you going to be?"

Pulling her up so she was kneeling on the bed, Dan clasped her tightly and crushed her against him, burrowing into the hollow of her throat with tantalizing kisses.

"I was hoping you'd dream up something fabulous for the two of us," he admitted between kisses. "You're so much more inventive than I am."

"Why don't you stick around and tell me more about it," she urged teasingly.

"Mmmm," he murmured. "I wish I could. You're almost irresistible."

"Just 'almost'?" Valerie challenged.

"Come on, Val," Dan protested, breaking away reluctantly. "You're not playing fair. You know I have to go to the hospital. But what do you say about Saturday night? Do we have a date?"

Sinking back into the bed, she pulled the sheet around herself and leaned against the pillows as if thinking intently about her answer. Finally, when he'd just about given up all hope of a positive reply, she said, "It might be an interesting night, after all."

"Then, you'll come?" he asked happily.

"On one condition," she said. "I decide our costumes."

"Okay," Dan agreed, "as long as you promise not to make me look like a fool."

"No conditions," she insisted with a sly smile curling the corners of her mouth. "After all, you said I was the inventive one."

It was noon before Valerie finally decided to drag herself into the shower. Her furtive mind had created dozens of schemes, but she had finally rejected them all. How was she going to deal with the masquerade party? During the weeks that she'd been seeing Dan, she had also been dating Bob. Unquestionably, both Bob and Dan would be at the party. They weren't just colleagues, they were friends as well, which made for a very awkward triangle. The safest thing to do would be to come down with a twenty-four-hour virus Saturday morning, and avoid the situation entirely. But what if Kim was there? Valerie had heard gossip recently that she and Karl Strausfield had become somewhat of an item. There was no way in the world Valerie was going to allow Dan to go to a party alone if there was the slightest chance that Kim would be there, too. With or without a date, Kim would seize any opportunity to win Dan back.

Tucking her hair into a shower cap, Valerie turned on the steaming water. She wasn't going to be foolish enough to go to a masquerade party in any of the traditional costumes. King, queen, clown, hobo, rabbit . . . She wanted to be something exotic—something that would show off her figure and show up all the other women there, particularly Kim, with her eight-month-pregnant figure.

Just thinking about the other woman made Valerie's blood boil. Kim had managed to insinuate herself into Dan's life so completely; it was almost impossible for any other woman to take her place. *The way to a man's heart is through his kids*, she thought bitterly. And Kim had both Betsy and Emily wrapped around her little finger.

When she'd promised not to see Dan any more, Valerie had won a lot of points with Betsy. But now that she and Dan were back together, Valerie was afraid Betsy would be more resentful than ever unless she could draw the young girl into their life, involve her in their relationship.

"I've got it," Valerie blurted aloud to herself. A satisfied smirk wreathed her face. Every kid loved a masquerade. So why not ask Betsy's help designing the costumes? Valerie knew exactly what she and Dan were going to be, but it would be easy enough to plant the idea in Betsy's head and let her believe it was her very own. Dan would be surprised and pleased that Valerie thought to involve Betsy, and the child would feel very important and very grown-up. Either way, Valerie told herself triumphantly, she'd win and Kim would lose. At last!

Cradling the phone against her shoulder, Natalie Hughes flipped through the stack of letters she was expected to type before lunch and waited for her call to go through. Although she was one secretary in a pool of four, she was being paid like an executive. Thanks to Jay Stallings, her silence truly was golden.

"Mr. Tom Hughes, please," she said crisply into the receiver. There had been a time when she used to call the office of Thomas Hughes, Attorney-at-Law, five or six times a day. He had been married to Carol then, and Natalie had been one of his clients. It hadn't taken her long to become his favorite client. Usually he worked on her case after office hours—at night, in her apartment.

After he'd divorced Carol and married her, everything had changed. Natalie had lied to him and cheated on him. But now that he'd had time to get over his anger, she thought, anything was possible . . . even a reconciliation. Legally, at least, Natalie was still Mrs. Thomas Hughes. After she packed her bags and left, Tom never pressed her for a divorce. Natalie hoped it was because he, too, wanted a reconciliation.

"Yes," Natalie answered the secretary on the other end of the phone, "you can tell him it's Mrs. Hughes—his wife."

Natalie expected an interminable wait. Instead, Tom came on the line immediately. "Hughes speaking," he said in his best attorney's voice.

"Hughes speaking on this end, too," she purred back in a voice that could melt ice.

"God, Natalie, it really is you," he sputtered. "I thought it was somebody playing a joke. What do you want from me now?"

"Can't a wife call her own husband anymore?" Natalie forced a hurt tone into her words. "I haven't talked to you in so long."

"Not long enough," Tom snapped quickly. Just hearing his wife's voice was enough to make him see red. Tom had thought he'd gotten over her, but the residue of anger burned like a forest fire in a drought.

Tom's reply was loud and clear, but Natalie pretended not to hear it. Rushing on as though he hadn't spoken, she said, "I know this will come as a surprise for you, but you'll never guess where I'm living now. Right back here in Oakdale. And I'm working—in real estate, of all things. I'm with Gar Kramer. Maybe you've heard of him. He's—"

"He's the biggest real estate broker in town," Tom interrupted, unable to disguise the surprise in his voice, "and one of the most questionable ones ethically. So you should fit right in there, Natalie," he added sarcastically.

"Tom," she murmured with false contriteness. "You're not being fair."

"When were you ever fair to me?" he demanded in a tight, angry voice. "You lied to me *before* we were married and you cheated on me *after* we were married. Now you expect me to be happy for you, even interested in you? Well, the truth is I don't give a damn where you're living or what you're doing."

"I thought that after all this time apart, you'd at least forgive me and maybe even miss me a little." Her voice was as cool and smooth as satin sheets. "I know *I've* missed *you;* you can't imagine how much. Each day without you—"

"Cut the nonsense, Natalie," he burst in explosively. "You've never cared about me and we both know it."

"How can you say such a thing, or even think it?" Her voice sank to an intimate whisper. No matter how difficult Tom was being, she wasn't ready to give up. "Of course I care about you. I love you; you're my husband. Now that I'm back in Oakdale, there's no reason to let old bitterness and past resentments keep us apart. We've meant too much to each other to let that happen. We should get together to clear the air between us. What do you say, Tom?" she coaxed in her most persuasive voice. "Let's have dinner tomorrow night and talk. You know, we can pour our hearts out. Give me a chance to show you that I really am sincerely sorry."

A bleak silence answered her pleading words, a silence so long that she began to think the line had gone dead. Then Tom answered, his voice sounding like an ominous echo, low, quiet, and implacable. "Now that you're back in Oakdale, Natalie, you can get yourself a lawyer. If you haven't filed for divorce by tomorrow morning, then I intend to sue you on grounds of adultery and desertion. I swear I will, and what's more, I'll take exquisite pleasure in doing it. When I'm through with you, you'll wish you never dared to come back to Oakdale."

"I can't believe you're saying these things to me." A note of uncertainty made her voice waver. "At least let's talk over our problems like mature adults. If we can't be lovers again, we could be friends."

"Friends trust each other," he was quick to remind her. "I couldn't ever trust you again."

"But you would trust your precious Carol, wouldn't you," Natalie snapped, frustration making her reckless. She wasn't going to get her husband back, so it didn't matter any longer what she said. "You're such a fool. Even now you can't see what was right in front of your nose. What do you think Carol was doing all those nights you were with me? Sitting home knitting? She was with Jay Stallings. Do you really buy her story that she bumped into Jay the day after she kicked you out and married him two weeks later?"

"Shut up, Natalie," Tom hissed venomously. If she'd been within reach, he would have taken great satisfaction in slapping her smug, cynical face. "Shut your filthy mouth. You can't believe there's such a thing in this world as a good, decent, loving woman."

She laughed mockingly. "Go ahead, Tom; go right ahead being a fool. I don't think you'd be capable of anything more, even if you tried." The other secretaries in her pool had stopped typing to listen to her conversation, but Natalie ignored them completely.

"I'm hanging up now," Tom said, "and I expect you to do exactly what I told you. Get yourself a lawyer—a good one. You're going to need him if you expect to bleed a penny out of me."

Dropping the receiver onto the cradle before he had a chance to hang up on her, Natalie rested her chin on her hands and imagined

Tom raging around the office. Natalie took supreme satisfaction in knowing that she had turned the knife in her husband's heart. But even that wasn't enough, not for the insults he'd hurled at her—refusing even to see her or talk to her, demanding that she get a lawyer about a divorce.

Although she took a sheet of stationery and carefully inserted it into her typewriter, her mind was far from the letter she began to type. Her best-laid plans were faltering. Natalie had plotted her return to Oakdale like a military tactician advancing an army through a war zone. But nothing had worked out the way she'd anticipated.

Instead of a fat bank deposit gathering interest, she had to work nine to five for her exorbitant payoff. And instead of the security of being an attorney's wife, she was facing divorce court. The ex-Mrs. Thomas Hughes, Natalie thought coldly, and it was all Carol's fault. Not a day of their marriage had passed that Tom hadn't compared her to Carol . . . unfavorably. That was why he wouldn't take her back, not because of her lying or cheating.

Natalie's fingers pounded the typewriter keys in a staccato rhythm, hitting blindly, as her husband had struck out at her. No matter what he thought, Tom wasn't through with her yet. No man was going to throw her over and get away with it. One way or another she was going to get even with Tom—and Carol.

Chapter Eight
Behind the Masks

Mrs. Berger frowned as she opened the front door. She disliked unexpected company almost as much as she disliked Valerie. "Good afternoon, Mrs. Conway. I didn't know you were coming over today."

"I didn't know I needed an invitation," she replied sweetly. Shrewd enough to sense the older woman's disdain for her, Valerie didn't particularly care for Dan's housekeeper. But, realizing she needed as many allies as possible if she were ever to win over the girls, she consciously attempted to keep her usual sarcastic tone out of her voice. "Is Betsy here? I need to speak with her."

"She's not back from school yet," Mrs. Berger said. "I expect her at any moment though, so you're welcome to wait."

Valerie sensed that she really wasn't welcome but decided to wait anyway; she wasn't the type of woman who could be bullied by a housekeeper.

Mrs. Berger motioned Valerie into the den and took her fur coat, handling it as if it were something distasteful. Once she had departed, Valerie idly wandered about the room, observing every detail. The home was comfortable, she decided, and attractive, but it seemed so small compared to the farmhouse she was currently renovating. And how Dan put up with all the crayons and toys on the coffee table, she couldn't guess; if Mrs. Berger were *her* housekeeper, she would give her a lecture on maintaining an orderly home.

While Valerie was wondering if Dan had ever considered boarding school for the girls, Betsy entered the room. Though the young girl already had taken off her coat, Valerie noted that her hair was still windswept and her cheeks were flushed from the cold.

Actually the color in her cheeks was due to Mrs. Berger's news that Valerie was waiting for her. Swallowing the lump in her throat, Betsy had bravely marched from the kitchen into the den. But upon seeing the beautiful and intimidating woman before her, the courage she had mustered fled.

"You wanted to speak with me?" she asked timidly.

Having already anticipated Betsy's apprehension, Valerie nodded her head more vigorously than necessary. "Your father has invited me to a masquerade ball, and I need your help in choosing our costumes."

"A masquerade ball?" Betsy repeated warily. "But Halloween was weeks ago."

"I know, but a masquerade can be any time of the year. Will you help?" Valerie hoped her request sounded sincere.

"Well, I don't know how much help I can offer," she replied. "I'm just a kid."

"But you're so talented and clever when it comes to things like this. I love the drawings you did that are on the refrigerator."

"Really?" Betsy had never been complimented by Valerie and couldn't help but feel proud. Maybe Valerie wasn't so bad after all, she thought.

Valerie was amazed that her words had affected Betsy in such a positive way. Winning the girl over was going to be easier than she had anticipated.

"Now, let's see." Valerie raised her hand to her chin and pretended to be engrossed in thought. "Our costumes should match, of course. I want mine to be unique, flashy, and most importantly"—she winked at Betsy conspiratorially—"I want it to be flattering to my figure."

Betsy giggled, delighted that Valerie was opening up to her. "Maybe you could be a prince and princess," she suggested.

"No, that's been done before. But it's a good suggestion," she added hastily. "I was thinking that the costumes should be based on people of historic times—or prehistoric times, maybe." Valerie had already planned to be a cave woman, but she wanted to plant the seed in Betsy's mind so it would look as if the idea had been hers.

"But that's not original," Betsy said, shaking her head. "You and Uncle Dan can't be a cave man and cave woman."

Valerie frowned. She thought Betsy would love the idea; she hadn't counted on the girl's dismissing the concept so readily. Though Valerie loved the notion of being dressed in a skimpy fur sarong, she knew she had to come up with a new idea, or Betsy would realize that her advice wasn't really wanted.

"Well, do you have any other ideas?" Valerie said somewhat disappointedly.

Betsy's gaze circled the room. She hoped that something on the walls or on a shelf would give her inspiration. Her eyes rested on one of Emily's coloring books lying on the coffee table. It featured scenes from Colonial times and had a picture on the cover of Betsy Ross sewing a flag.

"How about this?" the young girl cried excitedly, pointing to the book.

"Betsy Ross?" Valerie asked with little enthusiasm. She couldn't picture herself dressed in a powdered wig and such an ungainly costume.

"No, that's not what I mean." Betsy sat

down on the floor by the coffee table and, after selecting the red and blue crayons, quickly sketched her idea on a blank piece of paper. "Here," she said proudly, handing the finished drawing to Valerie.

After carefully examining it, Valerie slowly nodded her head. This time Betsy really had come up with an idea that was everything Valerie wanted: unique, flashy, and flattering to her figure.

"I was right, Betsy," she said finally. "I knew you would come up with the perfect costumes."

The girl beamed at the praise.

Valerie was not only surprised that she liked Betsy's idea, but that she was beginning to like the child as well. Maybe Kim was right. Maybe she and Betsy really could be friends.

The main ballroom of the Oakdale Country Club was hung with multicolored crepe paper streamers and dotted with balloons. Flowers blossomed from every corner, and colored lights cast their radiant beams careening around the room. The musicians in the jazz combo were warming up for the dancing that was scheduled to begin within the hour. At one end of the room, where Karl Strausfield was greeting the costumed guests as they arrived, an open bar was set up. Beside it stretched a buffet table with a huge tiered cake as a centerpiece. Karl was dressed as an eighteenth-century gentleman in black satin knee breeches, white silk stockings, a brocade coat, and a powdered wig. Beside him, in a high black hat and flowing, floor-length cape, the Wicked Witch of the West cackled in a high, eerie voice that sent chills through the blood.

At the far end of the room, as removed from the bar as possible, a knight in decidedly tarnished armor popped a few mints into his mouth and turned to the lion at his right.

"There's something definitely wrong with your costume," he said, eyeing her through his visor with a critical stare.

"Now don't start picking on me," the lion responded with a plaintive roar. "Remember I'm king of the jungle, so you'd better watch out if you don't want your head bitten off."

"The trouble is," he went on, ignoring her warning, "that you make such a petite lion. It seems perfectly reasonable for you to be cowardly. A ninety-nine-pound lion *should* be scared out of her mane."

Susan Stewart harrumphed. "Well, you're no one to talk, John. You're not exactly the ideal knight in shining armor. In fact, the very idea is ludicrous," she jibed.

For once, John was in too good a mood to take offense. It was the first hospital function he'd attended since he'd been dismissed, and he was determined to be on his very best behavior. "I'm not supposed to be a knight in shining armor," he corrected wryly. "I'm a knight errant—the perfect disguise, don't you think?"

Both Susan and Pat Holland, who was seated on John's other side, burst out laughing. "You're utterly incorrigible, Dr. Dixon," Pat admitted with a shake of her head.

It had been a battle to convince him to be her date. At first he'd refused outright, insisting that he would never again go near Memorial Hospital or anything connected to it. But Pat Holland didn't give up easily. Ever since the night she'd appeared on his doorstep, she'd been worming her way into his life by offering to help with his cardiology textbook and doing research and typing.

"I wonder who the hideous witch with Strausfield is." Susan was squinting through her lion's head, trying to identify all the guests.

"You mean you can't guess?" Pat flicked her fan and cast a furtive glance at John. His helmet hid the grim expression that tightened his features, and she couldn't resist an opportunity to gossip. "It could only be one person." Leaning across John, she mouthed the name in a hushed whisper. "Kim Dixon. John knows that she and Strausfield have been seeing a lot of each other lately. Oh, my, I don't believe it. Look who's coming in now."

All six eyes flashed to the door just in time to see the American flag breeze in. Dan Stewart, in a red and white union suit, was the stripes; Valerie Conway, in an electric-blue bodysuit, shimmered with fifty sequined stars. Both of them wore matching Uncle Sam top hats.

A year ago Susan would have been consumed with jealousy. But now that there was another man in her life—another man who meant so very much to her—she could look at Dan with another woman, even one as stunning and ostentatious as Valerie Conway, and keep her cool.

"Do you think he recognizes the witch?" Pat murmured, her eyes still glued to the scene at the door. "I'd give anything to be a fly on the wall over there . . . especially knowing what you did to them."

"What I did to *whom?*" Susan's voice was sharp and demanding. "I have no idea what you're talking about."

"It's okay, Susan," Pat whispered conspiratorially. "You don't have to play dumb with me. John told me all about the tape you erased."

"You did, did you!" Susan turned on John furiously, venom shooting from her eyes. "I told you about that tape in the strictest confidence, only because I was trying to help you with Kim. And you swore you would never —*never*—tell a soul. Now I find out what kind of a friend you really are, John Dixon. If you told Pat, you've probably blabbed to half of Oakdale as well."

110

John looked from one woman to the other in total confusion. He was sure he had never said a word about the erased tape to anyone. But if he hadn't and Susan hadn't, then how did Pat know? "No," he began tentatively, "it wasn't me. I don't know how Pat found out, but—"

"Of course you told me," Pat cut in brusquely. "Don't you remember? The night I dropped in on you unexpectedly. I brought a bottle of wine and we hashed over old times."

At the mention of the wine, John buried his helmeted head in his hands. That much he remembered all too painfully. He'd thought he could drink again, but he'd been wrong —terribly wrong. After the first glass of wine, the evening was a total blur. He had no idea what, if anything, had happened or what they'd talked about. All he remembered was coming to sometime in the early afternoon. Mary was helping him up off the floor, where he'd lain unconscious for hours, and his head felt the size of a blimp. It was an anguishing way to discover that he was still an alcoholic, and probably always would be. That was why he'd chosen the table farthest away from the bar, and why he was gobbling up whole handfuls of candy to keep his hands and mouth busy.

"I don't remember exactly how the subject came up," Pat was saying, coyly fluttering her fan. Although she was dressed as Marie Antoinette, she was determined that if heads were going to roll, hers would not be among them.

"But you did tell me all about it. Kim taped a love letter to Dan on his answering machine and Susan—"

"For God's sake," Susan hissed sharply. "Shut up, Pat, before the whole hospital staff knows every detail. You've got a voice that could shatter glass, and a mouth to match it."

John found himself coming to Pat's defense. "No, Susan. It's not her fault. I thought I could drink again, so I had a few glasses of wine with Pat, and you know how it is. I don't remember what I did or said. All I can say now is I'm sorry—terribly, terribly sorry."

Though she was angry and guilty, Susan couldn't blame John. She knew what he'd been through, because she'd been there herself, and he was one of the few friends who hadn't abandoned her. She had to forgive John, but Pat was another story altogether.

"You're not getting up from this table, Pat Holland, until you swear never to divulge a word that John told you," Susan warned ominously.

"Don't tell me you're threatening somebody else, darling." Kevin came up beside her, carrying a heaping platter of hors d'oeuvres, which he placed in the center of the table for the four of them to share. "You're supposed to be a *cowardly* lion," he teased, taking his place beside her.

"Well at least a cowardly lion can be ravenously hungry," she answered, letting Kevin's words soothe her anger. She was still eyeing Pat as if she were a time bomb that could blow up at any moment. "What took you so long? It seemed as if you were gone for hours."

"Would you believe ten minutes?" Kevin corrected easily. Although outwardly he seemed unconcerned, there was a hint of tension behind his nonchalance, as though he were trying too hard to give an impression of disinterest. "First there was a line to get to the buffet table. Then, when I finally got to the front of the line, there was so much food to choose from that I couldn't decide what to take. So I settled on a little of everything."

"Looks like a wonderful choice." Pat beamed at him, thankful that he had arrived in time to deflect Susan's anger. "Everything looks so delicious, I don't know what to try first."

Kevin reached for a sparerib and munched on it thoughtfully. "I also bumped into Sandy Garrison. I'm telling you, Susan, just so you won't read any secret, sinister meanings into it. She's here with Bob Hughes." The party was the first time that Susan and Kevin had been together since she'd abruptly disrupted his dinner with Sandy, and he didn't want anything to spoil their evening.

"Now, that's news," Pat chimed in before Susan had a chance to respond. "I heard that Dr. Hughes has his eye on Valerie Conway, even though she and Dr. Stewart have been a pretty steady item. Or maybe I should say *were* a steady item. Just look what's happening out there on the dance floor," Pat exclaimed breathlessly.

All heads turned to the center of the room. The band had begun playing and several couples were already dancing. Bob had maneuvered Sandy across the floor so that they were practically brushing shoulders with Dan and Valerie. A second later, Bob tapped Dan on the shoulder and the two men exchanged partners. Bob swept Valerie into his arms, dancing her away without missing a beat.

"I thought it was the stars and stripes forever," Susan quipped caustically. At the same time she sought Kevin's hand under the table and squeezed it in a silent message that the past was past.

Out on the dance floor, Dan led Sandy expertly through the steps of a fox-trot, but his body was rigid, and his eyes were glued to Bob and Valerie across the room. Over Sandy's head, he watched his old friend more intently than the woman he held so tenderly in his arms. Bob was laughing and talking animatedly, his eyes fixed on Valerie as if he'd forgotten there was anyone else in the room, anyone else in the world except her.

Hurt to have Bob brush her aside but determined not to show it, Sandy was chattering brightly, asking Dan how Betsy and Emily were. But he was concentrating so completely on the other dancers, he didn't even hear what she was saying. Finally, annoyed to find herself trapped in the center of an obvious triangle and ignored by both men, Sandy decided to make her presence felt. Swinging around somewhat awkwardly, Sandy forced Dan to turn his back on the other couple.

"I was asking you, Dan," Sandy reminded him loudly, "how Betsy and Emily are doing."

"I'm sorry." His downcast expression was so contrite that Sandy immediately regretted what she'd done. "I guess I forgot where I was for a moment," he said. "I hope you're not offended."

Sandy found herself shaking her head. It was impossible to stay angry with a man as handsome and charming as Dr. Dan Stewart. When the music stopped, he steered her across the room toward Valerie and Bob, who seemed unaware that the band had ceased playing.

When Valerie saw them approaching, she leaned into Bob more closely and gave him a warm hug. "Thanks for the dance, Bob," she said, loudly enough for Dan to hear clearly. "I hope we can do it again before the night's over."

"How about the next dance?" Bob suggested without hesitation.

"Sorry, Bob," Sandy cut in firmly, "the next dance is mine. That's the price you've got to pay for bringing me here tonight."

"It's not a price, Sandy, it's a pleasure," he replied smoothly as Dan placed a proprietary hand on Valerie's arm. "I'll get back to you very soon, Val," he promised good-naturedly.

Switching partners again, Bob and Sandy began to dance. But Dan led Valerie away.

"Where are we going, darling?" she asked with a petulant pout. "I thought you wanted to dance with me."

"Right now I want to talk to you, Valerie," he answered tightly.

"You sound so serious. Have I done something wrong?" She looked up at him with an expression of hurt innocence.

"I don't know," he admitted. "Maybe I did something wrong, inviting you here tonight."

"What do you mean? I don't understand."

Grabbing two martinis from a passing waiter's tray, he gave her one and took a long swallow from the other. "I'm talking about you and Bob. I guess you must have seen a lot of him all those days you were giving me the brush-off."

Sipping her drink, Valerie smiled at him coyly over the rim of the glass. "Bob is a good friend, too. But I don't see what business that is of yours. I'm with you tonight, so why don't you relax and enjoy it."

Even as she was talking, Dan was shaking his head. "I guess I'm just not that kind of guy. Listen, Val, I don't know how it is with women. But Bob is one of my oldest buddies. He's a good friend personally, and a respected colleague professionally. I'm not going to get in his way."

The smile froze on her lips. "Exactly what do you mean by that?" she demanded.

"I was watching when you two were dancing a few minutes ago. I saw the way Bob looked at you, and I know he hasn't looked at any woman that way since his wife died." Dan drew in his breath sharply. "I'm bowing out, Valerie. I'm not going to get in Bob's way."

"Did I hear you right?" She stared at him incredulously. Indignation flashed in her eyes, glittering like the irridescent stars that festooned her outfit. "You're passing me on to Bob as if I were a magazine you'd finished reading."

"No, Valerie," he insisted vehemently. "I'm just stepping aside. I have too much regard for Bob to compete with him, for you or any other woman."

"You have so much regard for Bob." Her voice rose angrily. "How about me? Don't you think I should have something to say about who I go out with?"

"Do you mind if I join you?" Bob's deep, quiet voice sounded behind them. "I hope I'm not interrupting anything."

Swiveling around to face him, Valerie glared from one man to the other. "As a matter of fact, you're just the man I wanted to see. If you think I'm your private property, you can wipe that idea right out of your head, Bob Hughes. I'm not ready to date any man exclusively. Is that perfectly clear? And as for you, Dan Stewart," she added, turning on him with equal fury, "I resent being passed around between the two of you. I"—she jabbed a long red nail at her chest for emphasis—"*I* will decide who I'm going to date, and when. And if I decide to try every man in Oakdale, it's none of your business. Do I make myself perfectly clear?"

Dan swallowed and fixed his eyes at some distant spot over her left shoulder, realizing as he did that he was staring at the peak of Kim's witch's hat. "I think I get your drift, Valerie. Now, if you'll both excuse me . . ."

Before she could utter a word of protest, Dan walked away, leaving her alone with Bob.

"I'm sorry, Val. I hope I didn't cause a problem between you and Dan by cutting in," Bob began.

Before Valerie could respond, Sandy was tugging at the sleeve of Bob's pirate shirt. "Sorry to steal him away," she said brightly. "But Bob did promise me the next dance, and the band is tuning up again."

"Don't go away," Bob called over his shoulder.

Shrugging to indicate her indifference, Valerie watched them walk out to the dance floor, then she turned away. Still angry and resentful, she made her way toward the buffet table, where Kevin Thompson was busily refilling a platter for his table.

"I like a man with a hearty appetite," Valerie quipped sarcastically.

"Don't get the wrong idea." Kevin laughed. "I'm not this big of a hog . . . at least not in public. By the way, Valerie," he added, casting an admiring glance down the length of her revealing bodysuit, "you look absolutely spectacular tonight. I can guarantee that Memorial has never seen anything to top that star-studded costume."

Picking up an egg roll, she bit into it tentatively. "Lot of good it's doing me," she answered glumly.

"Why the long face? A few minutes ago I saw you dancing and you looked like you were having a terrific time. You and Dan make quite a couple."

"*Made*," Valerie corrected.

Kevin was ready to come back with a caustic remark, but the expression on Valerie's face gave him pause. He'd never seen her look so upset. Usually she appeared as glamorous and untouchable as a cover girl. But now her eyes were glittering in a pool of tears that threatened to overflow at any moment.

"Valerie," Kevin said softly, "what's the matter? Can I do anything?"

"No." She shook her head and bit her lips to hold back the tears. "I'm sorry, Kevin. It's nothing . . . really, it's nothing."

"Come on," he said, taking her arm. "Let's get a breath of fresh air. It does wonders to clear away bad feelings and dry up unwanted tears."

With a grateful little smile, Valerie allowed him to lead her out to the deserted garden.

"Why don't you tell me about it, Valerie." Kevin's voice was soft but insistent. "It always helps to talk things out. That's what I tell Susan, and it works like a charm with her."

Valerie hesitated. "There's nothing to tell, really."

"Why don't you begin by telling me what happened between you and Dan? I swear to you, not a word of what you say will go any further. If you want, I'll forget you even spoke to me the minute we go back inside."

She gave a short, bitter laugh and turned away to hide the emotion she could no longer contain. "You know it's ironic. When I first moved to Oakdale, I thought Dan would be such a great catch. A handsome, rich, widowed doctor . . . and it didn't hurt, either, that Kim Dixon was interested in him. I wanted to snag him to hurt Kim, to get back at her for something she did to me a long time ago. That was in the beginning, and look at me now." Valerie's voice cracked, and Kevin waited quietly while she composed herself again.

"You and Dan look pretty good together as far as I can see," he said encouragingly.

"Looks are deceiving," she answered morosely. "Somewhere along the line I began to care about Dan—I mean *really* care about him. But you know what he told me tonight? Just because I've been dating Bob Hughes, too, Dan's decided to step out of the picture. He doesn't want to do anything to hurt his good friend Bob. It didn't matter that he might be hurting *me*."

Her voice dissolved into a plaintive cry that touched Kevin's heart. They'd all been wrong about Valerie Conway, he decided. She was more than a beautiful, scheming jet-setter. She was a woman who loved deeply and suffered painfully, just like any other human being.

"You know what I think you should do, Valerie?" he counseled kindly. "I think you should put on a fresh face, go right back in there to the party, and tell Dan exactly what's in your heart. If he knows the way you feel, he won't be so quick to turn you aside for any man, no matter how good a friend he may be. Besides," he added brightly, "I have it on very good authority that there's another woman in Bob's life. At least she's trying pretty hard to become a part of it again."

Batting her eyes to control her tears, she smoothed a few loose strands of her hair, patting them into place in preparation for her grand re-entry. "Do you really think it will make a difference if I tell Dan how I feel?"

"I really do," Kevin assured her, responding

warmly to the ring of hope that echoed in her voice. "I can't imagine a man not being flattered and thrilled to discover that Valerie Conway is eating her heart out over him."

"You're teasing, aren't you?" she asked defensively. More than anything else, Valerie didn't want to make a fool of herself in front of Dan. What if, by opening her heart to him, she scared him away?

Putting a protective arm around her, Kevin led her back to the party. "I'd never tease about a thing like that," he assured her with total sincerity. "Believe me, I wouldn't."

At one o'clock in the morning the band was playing its final number. Kevin closed his eyes and inhaled the fragrance of Susan's thick, lustrous hair. He felt her eyes fixed intently on his face and opened his own. "A penny for your thoughts," he murmured, pressing her closer. It was their first and last dance of the evening, and he wanted to prolong it forever.

"I was thinking about you," she answered, her tone quiet and serious.

"Something good, I hope."

"I was thinking about you and other women," she admitted readily.

Kissing the lobe of her ear, Kevin murmured contentedly, "There are no other women in the world except you."

"I've hardly seen you all night," she corrected. "Every other minute you were popping up from the table to rush off somewhere, and every time you finally came back, you said you'd been waylaid by a different attractive, unattached woman. Sandy Garrison, Valerie Conway . . ."

"Valerie isn't unattached at all," he informed her. "She's very much in love with Dan—that's what she confided in me."

Susan brightened in surprise. "I wonder where that leaves Kim. Did John tell you that he spilled the story of the infamous tape to Pat?"

Although the music went on, Kevin stopped abruptly. "Pat knows that you erased Kim's message to Dan?" he demanded in disbelief. "She's got the biggest mouth in Oakdale. Now you don't have any choice, Susan. You have to tell Dan and Kim what you did."

"I can never do that," Susan protested. The very thought of a confession brought butterflies to her stomach.

"You have to," Kevin insisted. A chord of steel which she had never heard before rang in his voice. She knew that this time there was no way she could talk her way out of it. "You have to promise me you will," he continued. "Too many people stand to be hurt by your silence. You can't manipulate people's hearts and lives like that. You can't be responsible for allowing them to decide their futures on misconceptions and deceit."

"All right, darling." She stroked his cheek

to calm him. He was more vehement than Susan ever remembered him. "We'll talk about it later. Right now I want—"

"No." He insisted, for once setting his own will firmly against hers. "There will be no tomorrow unless you own up to what you did. No matter how much I love you, I could never be happy knowing that you deliberately caused so much grief to so many others."

Susan's face turned a ghostly white. "Are you giving me an ultimatum, Kevin?" she murmured, shocked.

Meeting her searching gaze unswervingly, he answered with a curtness that made her tremble in his arms. "I'm giving you twenty-four hours to do the right thing. I know you want to, in your heart. You're just afraid and embarrassed. But I'll be right beside you all the way. You can count on that."

For what seemed like an eternity, she stood rigid in his arms while all the other dancers whirled around them. It was one of the most impossible decisions of her life. Susan knew what she should do, and she knew that Kevin was absolutely right. But her misgivings swirled in her mind like the dancing couples around her. Could she bring herself to confess? Did she have the courage to confront Dan and Kim with the truth? If she didn't, would she lose Kevin forever? The possibility hung over her head like a sharp blade. "I'll try, Kevin," she finally promised in a voice that quivered with apprehension. "But I think, in all fairness, I should warn John first. He's still hoping that he and Kim will be reunited after the baby is born. And this way—"

"Okay," Kevin agreed readily. "John is right over there at the coatroom getting his and Pat's things. You can tell him now, before you chicken out."

Pushing her out of his arms, Kevin watched as Susan marched determinedly across the room. She was breathless when she reached John and tugged on his arm. "I've got to talk to you," she whispered. "Now, before you go. It's urgent."

Seeing her white, taut face, John didn't hesitate. Backing into a corner with her, he studied her with concern. "What's the matter, Susan?" he questioned.

"It's the damn tape," she hissed. "Kevin has just given me twenty-four hours to admit the truth to Dan and Kim."

"He's what?" John asked incredulously.

"It's true. He's absolutely adamant on the subject. I have to tell them or I'll lose him—I just know I will!" Tears of frustration and fear welled in her eyes, but John wasn't moved at all.

As he listened to her, his eyes narrowed into angry slits and his face contorted with bitterness. "You can't, Susan," he ordered, "no matter what Kevin says. He's just bluffing, anyway."

"Not this time," she insisted, shaking her head hopelessly.

"Listen to me." John grabbed her fiercely by her lion's mane. "I won't allow you to go to Kim or Dan, is that clear? One word—one single word—and that will be the end of our friendship. If you tell them, you'll destroy any chance of happiness I still have with Kim. Don't you understand that?"

"But what about Kevin and me?" Susan was on the verge of tears. "If I don't tell them, what will happen to us? Kevin wasn't joking. I've never seen him more deadly serious in my life."

The club was emptying fast. Couples struggling to pull coats on over their costumes crowded in the foyer, exclaiming about how great the masquerade party had been. The food, the costumes, the music—better than any other year. Over Susan's shoulder, John caught a glimpse of a witch's hat at the front door. Just the peak was visible through the crowd, but it was enough to make his heart ache. No other woman—not Mary Ellison, not Pat Holland—could ever replace Kim in his heart, and he would never stop trying to lure her back. Never.

When he turned his attention back to Susan, his face was set even more grimly. "I know you can handle Kevin. Face it, Susan, he's crazy about you. And if you breathe a word about the tape to either Dan or my Kim, I'll get even with you, Susan."

Before Susan could answer, Pat sidled up to them, a curious expression lighting her painted face. "Come on, 'fess up," she said archly. "What am I missing? If you two are closeted together in a corner, I know it must be something juicy."

"Shut up, Pat." John shocked her into silence with his abruptness. Grabbing her by the elbow, he pulled her away from Susan. "Remember," he shot back over his shoulder, "a single word and you'll regret it. One way or another I'll get back at you, if it takes every day of the rest of my life."

Chapter Nine
True Confessions

It seemed to Valerie that the drive from the costume party back to her apartment was the shortest she'd ever taken. Dan maintained a relentless silence, his eyes glued to the road ahead. Although the night was clear, he concentrated as intently as though the road conditions were hazardous. Valerie opened her mouth a dozen times to give the little speech she'd prepared in the hours since talking to Kevin. But, each time, she bit her tongue before a single word escaped.

What if Dan laughed at her? What if she scared him away permanently? Worst of all, what if he was still in love with Kim? Then she'd make an utter fool of herself. These frightening questions were still spinning around in her brain, unanswered, when he pulled up sharply in front of her high-rise building.

"I can't believe we're here already," she murmured, finally breaking the silence between them. "Do you want to come up for a cup of coffee?"

"Not tonight, thanks," he answered, his hands still gripping the steering wheel, his eyes still staring straight ahead.

Valerie twisted the emerald ring that gleamed on her finger. "There is something I want to talk to you about, Dan. I was hoping you'd have a few minutes." She watched his face, scrutinizing it for some indication of what was going on in his mind. But his serious demeanor revealed nothing, not so much as a flicker of expression.

"Shoot," he said, glancing at her coolly. "What do you want to talk about?"

"Us." The short, potent word hung between them.

"You mean you and Bob?" Dan finally asked, breaking the uncomfortable silence.

Shaking her head, Valerie looked away, afraid to reveal her own vulnerability. "No," she replied in a husky whisper. "I mean Dan Stewart and Valerie Conway."

"I thought I made myself clear at the party," he answered evenly. "I'm out of that picture now."

Her hand clutched his arm, and he stiffened. Cutting her out of his life seemed to make him care for her even more. In his heart, he wanted to deny the words he'd just uttered.

"It's not that simple for me," Valerie murmured, saying the words he ached to hear. "I can't just write you out of my life."

"I'm not sure I know what you're getting at. Do you want to pit Bob and me against each other?" Although his tone was still distant, his hand strayed to where her fingers touched his arm.

"I want you to forget about Bob and concentrate on us—you and me, Dan." Her fingers tightened on his arm and she turned to face him. There was an urgency in her voice he hadn't heard before. "You may not want to hear this, but I'm going to tell you anyway, and you can laugh at me for saying it if you want to." Inhaling sharply, she took the plunge, praying in her heart that Kevin was right. "I don't want to say I'm in love with you, Dan, because I'm not sure what it is that makes me think about you all day, wonder what you're doing and whom you're with. All I know is that I've never felt this way about any other man."

Reaching for her hand, he squeezed it so tightly that a cry rose to Valerie's lips, but she stifled it. "I never thought—" he began.

"Please, Dan, don't think," she urged. "Just feel what I'm saying. I know I'm not always warm and open and generous with my emotions. A part of me, maybe the very deepest, most secret part, is still bitter and confused. A long time ago—way back when Kim was married to my brother Jason—there was another man in my life, a man named Cliff. I was crazy about him at the time. All I wanted in the world was to be his wife, but Kim and my brother had a different idea. And they didn't rest until they'd destroyed what Cliff and I had together. That's why, to this day, a part of me is unable to forgive and forget. A part of me is afraid to love again."

She was trembling from the anguish of remembering and the effort of confessing, of stripping bare her heart and soul. It had been so long since she'd allowed herself to feel anything deep and true and unselfish. Only Dan's hand tightly clutching hers steadied her.

Lifting her chin up to see for himself what was reflected in her eyes, he murmured huskily, "I had no idea, Val . . . no idea at all. I thought you were jealous of Kim because of what used to be between us."

A bittersweet smile hovered at the corners of her lips. "Kim and I go back a long way, and so does the bitterness between us."

"But don't you understand," he explained, searching her face to see if his words were reaching her, impressing her, "you can never be free to love me or anyone else again while your heart is so full of anger and resentment. You should talk to Kim, Val; listen to her side of the story. I can't believe that she would ever set out to destroy you. It just goes against everything she is, everything she believes."

Even as he spoke, Dan felt once more his desperate yearning for Kim, as if he had just held her in his arms an hour before. Would he ever be able to forget her—to replace her memory with Valerie or any other woman?

"Maybe you're right," Valerie admitted slowly. "Maybe I will talk to her, if you think I should. Maybe it would be better for all of us."

He smiled for the first time all evening, although his heart was being pulled in two directions, tugged back by an old love, pushed forward by a new desire. "I'm sure you won't regret it," he said, trying not to dwell on his own regrets.

"I hope you're right," she agreed thoughtfully. Somehow she had started out trying to let him see what was in her heart, and instead they were talking about Kim, the very person Valerie wanted him to forget. "But what about us?" she pressed. "Is this really the end of a perfect relationship?"

Dan tried to remember how good a friend Bob had always been, but Valerie was leaning toward him, her perfume filling the closed car hypnotically, her lips too close to resist. "Do you really mean what you said?" he asked huskily. "That you feel something special for me?"

"Something very special." She whispered the words against his cheek, tempting him with her closeness.

Thinking how close he had been to losing

her, Dan captured her lips with a kiss that reaffirmed his devotion to her. When they finally parted, they were both breathless.

"Now do you believe that you're special to me?" Valerie smiled seductively.

"I wouldn't mind if you repeated yourself," Dan teased.

"I will when we get upstairs," she whispered.

For a moment Dan hesitated. The temptation was too real to deny, but so was the friendship of a lifetime.

"I don't want this to be the end of anything," he explained, choosing his words carefully so as not to offend her, "but neither do I want to hurt anyone else by our happiness."

"I'm not sure I understand what you mean," she admitted, stunned that he was rejecting her after such a searing kiss.

"I want to see you again, Val. The week you wouldn't go out with me was pure hell," Dan admitted. "Every time you refused me, I felt as if a thick curtain of darkness were closing in on me, blocking every glimmer of brightness from my life. I know it must have been miserable for the girls, too. I was impossible to live with and, young as they are, they felt the difference in our home. Betsy, especially, seems sensitive to my mood swings. I think she blamed herself for coming between us."

"Well, there's no question that she feels a lot better about us than she used to," Valerie assured him, masking the annoyance she felt discussing his children now. She wanted Dan to take her in his arms, to make her believe they were the only two people in the world. "Letting her help with our costumes really made her feel important," she said with false enthusiasm. "Betsy and Emily will be fine. For now, why don't you concentrate all your attention on me."

"I'd like to spend the night," he replied hesitantly. "But I think we should take it slow and easy for a little while. There are so many people to think of besides ourselves—Betsy and Emily, Kim, Bob. I don't want to hurt them to secure our own happiness."

"What about the special way I feel for you?" Valerie asked, the pain clear in her voice. "Doesn't that account for anything?"

"It means a lot," he murmured, bringing her hand to his lips and kissing the open palm. "But if it's a true feeling, it will strengthen and deepen with time. And who knows? Anything could be possible then."

The promise, the suggestion, the hope lingered between them like an irridescent bubble, too fragile even to attempt to catch. But it was all Valerie had for comfort that night.

A glass bubble atop Oakdale's tallest skyscraper, The Atrium was a stunning restaurant, decorated in glass and chrome and known for its wide variety of quiches and salads. After much deliberation and a lengthy debate with herself, Valerie chose a vegetarian dish with lemon dressing. But except for an occasional nibble on a string bean, the lunch sat in front of her virtually untouched.

"That salad looks terrific, Valerie," Kim remarked. "I can't believe you've barely touched it." Her own chef's salad was already half-finished.

"I'm sure it is," Valerie replied tensely. "But the minute I saw food in front of me I suddenly lost my appetite. Does that ever happen to you?"

"Of course," Kim admitted readily. "When I'm upset or nervous about something, it's hard for me to work up an appetite. Is there anything wrong?"

"Not a thing," Valerie answered, too quickly to be convincing. "Why do you ask?"

"No special reason," Kim replied easily. "I just thought you might have invited me to lunch today for a particular reason, but I guess I was wrong."

Toying with a broccoli spear, Valerie eyed her uncertainly. "Actually," she began hesitantly, "there is a method to my madness. It was Dan's idea, really. He thinks it's about time you and I cleared the air between us, and I surprised myself by agreeing."

Kim could barely hide her astonishment. After all these bitter years, Valerie was ready to bury the hatchet and make peace? The very thought was mind-boggling. After living most

135

of her adult life with the knowledge that Valerie was her sworn enemy, Kim found it hard to believe that her former sister-in-law was finally ready to call a truce. "You're not serious, are you?" she asked skeptically.

Valerie nodded. "I have never been more serious about anything in my entire life." And she meant every word of it, though it wasn't as if she had changed overnight. Valerie still resented Kim as much as ever. But if making peace with her was the price she had to pay to win Dan over, then she was ready to go through the necessary motions.

"So you won't be holding a grudge against me anymore? Not even about Cliff?" The words were out of Kim's mouth before she realized what she was saying.

At the mention of his name, Valerie's face drained of color. "I guess you and I have to talk about Cliff," she admitted tensely.

Kim shook her head in disbelief. "But that was so many years ago, I can hardly remember what happened."

"Believe me," Valerie assured her with her familiar sharpness, "I can refresh your memory on every detail. Because I haven't forgotten a single thing about Cliff—or the way you turned him against me. If it hadn't been for you, he and I would be together now. Every single day of my life I live with that bitter memory. That's why I've hated you, Kim," she admitted, the old antagonism raising its ugly head like a cobra.

"No, Valerie," Kim said as gently as she could. "You and Cliff wouldn't be together now." Putting down her fork, she pushed her unfinished salad aside and considered the other woman thoughtfully. For so many years Kim had fulfilled her husband's final request and hidden the truth, afraid that it would shatter Valerie. But now she could see that, in her desire to spare Valerie's feelings, she had actually done much more harm than good. "I think the time has finally come to tell you what really happened between Cliff and your brother Jason."

"Not between Cliff and Jason," she corrected, the fury she'd harbored against Kim so long beginning to churn again. "Between Cliff and you."

Kim shook her head sadly. When she tried to look back now, she felt as if she were remembering a different person, a stranger. She had been so young when she exchanged wedding vows with Jason, and so young when he died. The grief that had seemed so intense at the time was too remote to cause even a twinge of pain now. But clearly it was different for Valerie. Those long-ago years of love and loss were still a very real, very poignant part of her life.

"Neither Jason nor I had any intention of

hurting you, Valerie," Kim said firmly. "It was Cliff who did it to you. If you really want me to tell you the truth about what happened, I will—but on one condition. You have to hear me out. Let me tell the story my own way without interruption."

"What do you want to do? Gag me?" she jibed, unable to control her own deep-seated bitterness.

Kim forced her voice to remain even. "I just want you to listen, Val. Listen with an open mind. Then you can say or do whatever you want, okay?"

The most Valerie could offer was a snide shrug, but it was enough to satisfy Kim. Dabbing her lips with her napkin, she rested her arms on the edge of the table and leaned closer to Valerie. "You'll have to bear with me for a few minutes, while I try to resurrect the old memories. It was such a long time ago. Looking back now, we seemed so young and vulnerable. Maybe that was the trouble."

Valerie frowned in answer. It was impossible to believe that Kim had forgotten the very things that burned as fiercely as ever in her own heart and still shaped her life. But for once she held her tongue.

"I'm not going to deny that Jason hated Cliff. When he heard that you were going to marry him, your brother saw red. I have to admit that I agreed with him completely. When you started dating Cliff, I made Jason back off, thinking that you would eventually wake up to the kind of guy he really was. Unfortunately, the old saying was true in your case. Cliff was the first man you'd ever loved and—believe me, Val—your love was very, very blind."

"What do you mean by that crack?" Valerie interrupted angrily.

Kim sighed so deeply it seemed as if it came from the very depths of her being. "I made Jason promise he wouldn't tell you this, because I was afraid the knowledge would hurt you too profoundly. But there's no point in trying to protect you anymore. Cliff wasn't the wonderful, warm, devoted guy you thought he was. He was a hopeless womanizer. He was a con man. He lived off women. When he dropped you off at night, he would turn right around, go back to the bars, and pick up somebody else."

"No!" Valerie denied hotly. But Kim didn't listen. She continued, as if she hadn't heard a thing.

"I began to be suspicious when Cliff made a pass at me. I was furious and shocked. You and I were best friends back then, besides the fact that I was already married to your brother. Cliff just laughed and called me a prude. I can still hear him: 'Don't worry about it. Val trusts me, and Jason trusts you, so we're home free. Neither of them will suspect a thing.'

"That night I told Jason he should find out

more about Cliff before you married him. It didn't take much digging to discover that Cliff had a virtual harem. He was engaged to half a dozen women, and he tapped each of them regularly for money. That's where his 'untold fortune' came from. He'd never been a race-car driver or an artist or any other of the romantic stories he filled your head with. He was a bum, pure and simple."

Valerie opened her mouth to interrupt, but Kim refused to stop until Val had heard it all.

"I didn't believe Cliff was like that, either, when Jason came home and told me. But he said he would prove it. The very next day he invited Cliff over and offered to give him five hundred dollars in cash if he would get out of your life." Kim shook her head slowly as she spoke, still disgusted by the memory. "I was hoping Cliff would refuse, but he didn't even hesitate. His eyes lit up greedily. 'Make it a grand,' he bargained, 'and I won't just bow out of your sister's life, I'll blow town altogether. Val must be worth that much to you, and I can go to Vegas with big money to play with. Have you seen the showgirls there?' He winked slyly at Jason.

"I turned away, too sickened to listen any longer. Jason and I had saved exactly one thousand twenty-three dollars, but he never hesitated. He wrote Cliff a check that night. 'Take it and get out before I kill you,' he said in a voice I'd never heard him use before."

For a long moment, Kim paused, the raw emotional power of that moment coming back to her. She never doubted that Jason would be as good as his word. "Jason wanted to tell you exactly what happened, but I wouldn't let him. I didn't want you to hate your brother for what he'd done, and I didn't want you to be shattered by Cliff's deceit. You were so young and vulnerable." She shook her head, remembering the heartbreak of it all.

"Cliff was the first great love of your life. At least that's what you believed. If you discovered that all the time he'd been using you, taking advantage of your love as he did to so many other women, I was afraid your ego would be destroyed. How could you ever trust another man again? Jason finally agreed with me, and we never told you the truth."

Kim smiled sadly before continuing. "Of course, you stopped at nothing to learn why Cliff had left you, and soon you learned that Jason and I were involved. I didn't want you to hate Jason, so I took the responsibility for the whole ugly business. But we never told you about Cliff's infidelities, and when Jason was on his deathbed he made me promise I never would.

"So, in trying to protect you and keep my vow to Jason, I kept the truth hidden all these years. I realize now it was a mistake. I lost you as a friend and you've never gotten over Cliff. You built him up in your mind to be such a god that you've never been free to fall in love again. No man could ever measure up to the image of Cliff you've invented. As a result, you've filled your heart with bitterness and resentment, instead of opening it to a new honest love, new possibilities. I'm sorry, Val," Kim finished softly. "I hope, at the very least, you'll believe that."

Looking across the table and meeting Valerie's eyes for the first time since she began her story, Kim was surprised to see a mist shimmering in her former sister-in-law's eyes.

Valerie had agreed to have it out with Kim only to impress Dan. But now she realized how unfair she'd been. She and Kim had been friends once . . . maybe they could be again.

"You're wrong about one thing, Kim," she said, a smile glinting through the tears. "I've finally met a man who is more wonderful than any dream."

"Dan?" Kim murmured, biting her trembling lip to keep it from betraying the love that still burned inside her.

Nodding, Valerie dabbed at the corner of her eyes with her napkin. "I'm afraid to believe it myself, but I love him. I've never felt like this about anyone—not even Cliff. Maybe I shouldn't be telling you this, because I know there used to be something between the two of you."

"Used to," Kim echoed, closing her mind to the cry that was searing her heart. "But he needs someone, Val, and so do Betsy and Emily. I'm glad that someone is you."

"Will you help me with the girls?" she asked. "I know how much you mean to them."

It took all her strength, but Kim answered from the bottom of her heart. "Of course, Val. I'd do anything in the world to make those two little girls happy again."

Chapter Ten
Telling Secrets

Wiping the hair back from her moist forehead with the sleeve of her maternity smock, Kim admired her handiwork. Pastel-colored stencils straight from the pages of Mother Goose formed a border around the sides of an old toy chest. Tired from the exacting work but pleased with the happy results, she began to clean up her patterns and paints.

The nursery was almost finished. The pale lemon walls were newly painted and now gaily decorated. A cornflower-blue wall-to-wall carpet had been laid a few weeks earlier. A bassinet covered in a pale yellow ruffled skirt and hood was pushed in the center of the room, together with a changing table, chest of drawers, and antique rocking chair in which Kim's own mother had lulled her to sleep.

Looking around the room, Kim made a mental list of what she still had to do—arrange the furniture, make up the bassinet, put up curtains . . . As her glance lingered at the bare window, she found herself staring more intently. A steel-gray sedan was pulling up in front of her door. Kim watched in surprise as the car door opened and Susan got out. Susan had always been John's friend, not hers, so it came as quite a shock to see her approaching the house.

Before she reached the steps, Susan hesitated, as if she couldn't make up her mind whether to go up to the door or turn around and get back in the car. Finally, while Kim watched, Susan squared her shoulders and rang the bell.

It took Kim a few moments to extricate herself from the stencils and brushes and to answer the door—time enough for Susan to think about what she was doing. Difficult though it was, there was no doubt in her mind that she had to go through with her plan, regardless of what John thought of her or how deeply hurt she was by his threats. It wasn't only that Kevin was pressing her so relentlessly to confess once and for all; her own conscience was urging her to come clean.

But she could never, ever confess to Dan. There was absolutely no question. To go to her ex-husband and explain what she had done —and why—was impossible. How could she tell him that she had erased his answering-machine tape because she was jealous of Kim, because she didn't want another woman to take her place and become the new Mrs. Dan Stewart?

But, driven by guilt and by the fear of losing Kevin, Susan was prepared to make a clean breast of everything to Kim—if she could bring herself to go through with it. . . . There was no time left, though, to chicken out, because Kim was already opening the door.

"Well, this really is a surprise," she said, welcoming Susan with her usual gracious smile. "Come in. I've been fixing up the baby's room and I was about to treat myself to a break. You're just in time to join me. Would you like to be formal and wait in the living room, or would you just as soon come along to the kitchen with me?"

"The kitchen sounds fine," Susan agreed readily. The last thing she wanted was to make a production of her visit. In fact, with every step she was beginning to wish that she hadn't come. She would find some way to live with the gnawing guilt and convince Kevin that telling her secret at this point would do more harm than good. Whatever had been between Dan and Kim was probably over and done with. Both of them had carved new directions for their lives just as she herself had—Dan with Valerie, and now Kim with Karl. John didn't want to believe that Kim could ever be serious about Karl, but there was no question he was interested.

"What would you like? Coffee, tea, or hot

chocolate?" Kim was asking, drawing Susan away from her own doubts.

"Hot chocolate, if it's not too much trouble," she answered tentatively.

"Terrific." Kim laughed. "I was hoping you'd say that. Now I have a legitimate excuse to indulge my craving for chocolate."

In minutes she mixed the cocoa, sugar, and milk. While it was warming, she beat a bowl of heavy cream to put on top. Watching Kim's quick, sure movements, Susan was surprised to see how graceful she was. Her own pregnancy with Emily had been a nightmare.

After placing two steaming mugs of cocoa on the table and a plate of oatmeal cookies between them, Kim sat down opposite Susan. "I can't tell you how glad I am you stopped by. I had the worst craving for hot chocolate, and I never would have made it for myself. Probably after the baby is born and I'm still as big as a house, I'll wish I hadn't indulged myself," she said, stirring a heaping spoonful of cream into the cocoa. "But right now I feel absolutely wicked."

Reaching for a cookie more from nervousness than from hunger, Susan looked at her in disbelief. "I wish I didn't have anything more than a cup of cocoa to feel wicked about."

Kim laughed. "You shouldn't feel wicked. You should feel absolutely terrific about yourself. The way you've straightened yourself out after all the problems you've had is an example for all of us. I hope John will do as well as you have."

Spooning the whipped cream off the top of the chocolate before it dissolved entirely, Susan glanced over at Kim. "I'm not so sure you'd be saying that," she admitted slowly, "if you knew what brought me here today."

"I can't deny I'm curious," she owned up readily. "You're welcome to visit anytime," she hurried to add, "but you've always been more of a friend to John than to me. That's why I'm surprised to have you sitting here at my kitchen table."

Susan knew it was now or never. Still, she wasn't sure that she had the courage to tell Kim the truth. Tiny beads of sweat broke out on her forehead at the mere thought of it. What would Kim say? What would she do? What if the shocking news caused her to go into premature labor? Susan was tempted to make up a reason for her visit, but the thought of Kevin kept her from going home. He was so uncompromising, so adamant, that Susan was afraid to go back without making a full confession.

"Actually," she began tentatively, "I came to tell you a secret."

"Tell me a secret?" Kim echoed curiously. "Something good, I hope, though I can't imagine what it could be."

Even as Kim was talking, Susan was shaking her head. Now that she'd taken the plunge, there was no way to turn back. "I'm afraid what I have to say may shock you, Kim," she admitted tensely. "And I certainly don't want to upset you in your condition."

"Don't worry about me. My doctor says I'm strong enough to play professional football." Although Kim tried to joke, the banter sounded forced and artificial. "I guess you'd better come right out and tell me straight, Susan," she admitted. "Otherwise one of us is going to—"

"It's about you and my ex-husband," she broke in before Kim had a chance to finish.

"About Dan and me?" Kim couldn't believe Susan was serious. "I've scarcely seen Dan since . . . since he went to South America. And then it's only been for a moment—at the masquerade party, for instance." The mere mention of Dan's name sent her heart thumping and the color flooding her cheeks. There would never be another man in her life—there probably wasn't one in the entire universe —who could fill the void his loss created.

"That's what I'm talking about," Susan insisted. But the more she talked, the less sense she made to Kim. "I have to tell you about something that happened before Dan went away . . . something that I'm afraid may have changed your life—and a lot of other people's lives, too."

In her nervousness, Susan was revolving the cocoa mug between her hands, keeping it, and herself, in perpetual motion. Her eyes darted around the room, resting for a split second on the polished copper molds hanging on the wall beside the range; on the ceramic clock, which Kim had painted herself with pictures of different fruits and vegetables; on the row of canisters, each one shaped like a different old-fashioned store. Her eyes rested, but they didn't register.

"I can't imagine what you're talking about," Kim protested. A part of her was waiting, every nerve end on alert, for Susan to go on. But another part wished she'd just go away without another word. Kim believed that her chance for happiness with Dan was lost. Why dredge up a past that could never become the glorious future they'd dreamed of? What good would it do either of them now? "And to tell you the truth," she added, "I'm not sure that I want to know."

Nibbling nervously on the cookie she'd forgotten she'd taken, Susan wondered again whom she was helping and whom she was hurting by her confession. But Kevin was so sure that it was the right thing to do, and her own guilt was so persistent, nagging her like a chronic ache, that she had to tell Kim the whole truth—regardless of the consequences.

"I have to tell you, even though when I'm finished you may wish I'd kept my mouth shut. It's about that time when you and Dan broke up. Remember? You were back with John recovering from your amnesia, and Dan was packing the two girls off on their South American trek."

Kim only nodded in answer. How could she ever forget the most heartbreaking moments of her life? She glanced at Susan and saw the taut lines of tension that pinched her face. Then she turned away quickly, unwilling to reveal the depth of her own anxiety.

Susan's hands tightened around the mug. She took a deep breath and plunged into the murky waters of past deceptions. "Around that time you tried to call Dan, but all you could reach was his answering machine. I imagine you must have tried a couple of times, then left the message in a desperate, last-ditch effort to reach him before he left Oakdale—maybe permanently."

"The tape . . ." Kim murmured in a shocked whisper. But Susan either didn't hear her or was so bent on getting it all out at last that she couldn't stop herself now.

"It's the only reason I can think of for putting your most personal thoughts and intimate feelings on a—"

"How do you know what was on that tape?" Kim cut in so sharply, with such a cutting, demanding edge in her voice that Susan stopped short. "And don't tell me Dan let you listen to it, because I'd never believe that for a moment. He's not that kind of man."

"No, he's not," Susan admitted. Her voice

dropped to a hesitant murmur. She'd expected Kim to get angry, to weep and scream. But the cold ferocity of her response came as a stunning surprise. "I went to say good-bye to Emily, but Dan had the girls out shopping for their trip. While I was waiting for them to get back, I wandered into the den. It just happened to be at the exact moment that you were taping your message."

Kim stared at her, so incredulous that she was absolutely speechless. Susan rushed ahead with her story, eager to tell her secret and clear her conscience once and for all, as cleanly as she had cleared the tape.

"I'm sorry, Kim," she murmured. "If it happened now, I would never interfere. But back then, I was still crazy about Dan. Ridiculous as it may sound to you, I honestly believed that I had a chance to get him back—as long as you were out of the picture. Dan was so in love with you, and so heartsick thinking that you didn't remember him. If he'd ever heard that tape, he would have canceled his trip and killed John if he had to, to get to you. No one and nothing in the world could have kept him from you."

Susan paused to try to steady herself, but it was a hopeless cause. Her hands, her knees, her voice were trembling uncontrollably. "I guess I acted out of desperation . . . on a moment's impulse, knowing how deeply Dan loved you and wanting him still for myself. The erase button was at my fingertips. All I had to do was push it and I'd wipe you out of his life permanently. He'd leave on his trip, convinced that you'd forgotten him. You'd believe that he didn't care anymore—that he got your message and left town anyway. And no one would ever know what I had done."

A small gasp escaped from Kim's dry lips. "No, Susan! You couldn't have." Although she was listening to every word Susan spoke as intently as she had ever listened to anyone in her life, she couldn't believe her own ears.

"I'm sorry, Kim—truly sorry." Guilty tears strangled Susan's voice. If she had hoped that the passage of time would have eased Kim's grief, she was wrong—terribly, terribly wrong. "I know it doesn't help to say this, but believe me, if I had it to do over, I'd never interfere in your lives."

Kim was shaking her head as if she still couldn't believe what Susan had done. For so many lonesome days and desperate nights, she'd tortured herself thinking that Dan didn't love her anymore—that he didn't even care enough to answer her call. And now, when she was finally beginning to build a new life for herself, to discover that their love had been destroyed, their chance for happiness wiped out by the press of a single button.

"Does Dan know?" she finally managed to murmur in a strangled voice.

Susan looked down at her half-empty mug, the chocolate now crusted and cold and unappetizing. She couldn't face the anguish that etched Kim's face. "Kevin wants me to tell him," she admitted, "but I can't. If it were anyone but Dan—"

"If it were anyone but Dan, you would never have erased the tape," Kim accused with a bitter edge in her voice. Coming from Kim, it was almost as shocking as her own confession. Secretly Susan had always envied Kim's seemingly limitless capacity for compassion and understanding. She always seemed to find some explanation, some rationale, for even the most selfish, hateful behavior. But this time her well of compassion seemed to have run dry where Susan was concerned.

"I can't deny that, Kim," Susan admitted. "You know how I used to feel about him. Dan was my whole world. Even after he left me, I could only think of how to get him back. That's why I sued for custody of Emily. I never wanted to be responsible for a child. I just thought I could force Dan to come back. When that backfired, when you moved in, clearly destined to take my place, I got desperate. I think at that point in my life I would have done anything—*anything*—to keep Dan from marrying you."

Closing her eyes to shut out Susan, the agony of fate, and the sudden contractions that stabbed like knife wounds, Kim fought to hold fast to the slender thread of control that kept her from crumbling completely. All the could-have-beens that Susan erased with the tape flooded her mind. She and Dan could have been married by now. She could have been a real mother to Betsy and Emily instead of a secret friend. And, most heart-wrenching of all, the baby kicking her stomach so persistently could have been Dan's. Instead of decorating a nursery alone, she and Dan would be waiting and planning together for their new arrival. Instead . . .

Opening her eyes, she stared at Susan with a directness that demanded the total truth. "Are you telling me that Dan still doesn't know anything about my tape?"

Susan looked away, tears of remorse stinging her eyes. All she could think of was how totally lost she'd feel if Kevin were suddenly cut out of her life. For the first time since erasing the tape, she put herself in Kim's place.

"Dan doesn't even know you tried to call him. He has no idea a message even existed. I know I should confess to him, just as openly and honestly as I'm confessing to you, but I can't face him. He'll be so wild with fury, I don't know what he'd do if he heard it from me. We're on good terms now, but all it would take is something like this for him to keep me from Emily." Susan hesitated, knowing that she had no right to ask Kim for a favor and even less right to expect a favorable answer. "I thought I'd leave it up to you. I've done enough damage to your life already. If you want Dan to know, I think you should be the one to tell him. And if you don't want him to know, you can be absolutely sure that I'll never breathe a word about it." Raising her right hand, Susan swore as solemnly as if she were testifying in court.

But her promise fell on deaf ears. Kim's mind was caught on Susan's previous words. *"If you want Dan to know . . ."* When her amnesia had finally lifted, the memories of Dan had flooded back with even more clarity and vividness. It almost seemed as though the longer they were apart, the brighter the memories grew. Each day, each hour they had spent together, tramping through snowy woods with Emily and Betsy or entwined in each other's arms in the ecstasy of love, was implanted in her consciousness with the freshness and immediacy of an instant replay.

How could Dan believe she didn't remember when every moment they spent together —every touch, every kiss, every caress—was burned in her memory for all eternity? Susan's words returned again and again like a haunting melody: *"If you want Dan to know . . . If you want Dan to know . . ."*

The afternoon sun streamed through the kitchen window, giving the lie to dreary December weather and making the copper molds gleam like freshly minted pennies. Kim didn't notice. Now that Susan had finally gone, the anguished grief that she'd forced herself to hold back swept over her like a tidal wave. Burying her face in her hands, she put her head down on the kitchen table and wept her heart out. Alone, with no one to offer comfort, no one to urge restraint, she didn't have to try to control her grief or slow her tears.

It seemed so incredible, so unjust, that a single vicious action could deny Dan and her a life of happiness. And the worst of it was, Dan didn't even know. She couldn't allow him to go on thinking that she had forgotten him, that some perverse part of her brain had wiped out his love. No matter how diverse their futures were, Kim wanted Dan at least to know the truth. His love had been the most glorious, all-consuming experience of her life. Even if it was just a memory, it was one to which she held fast and cherished above all others.

When the sobs that racked her body quieted, she went over to the sink and splashed cold water on her swollen face. Cupping the icy water in her hands, she blinked into it to stanch the flow of tears and soothe the redness. Once her mind was made up, Kim moved with grim purpose. She had to make herself presentable to go to Dan's office. One maternity dress was as unflattering as the next, so she didn't bother to change her clothes. She concentrated instead on her hair and makeup.

Arriving at Dan's office half an hour later, Kim found herself facing an exodus. As she was trying to get into his waiting room, a procession of a dozen patients was streaming out.

"Mrs. Dixon!" Dan's nurse looked up from her desk in surprise. "I haven't seen you in a thousand years."

"It does seem that long, doesn't it," Kim agreed dryly. "I was hoping I could see Dr. Stewart for a few minutes, if you can squeeze me in. It's nothing urgent," she added quickly, afraid to alarm the nurse, "but—"

"Dr. Stewart has been called to surgery. I had to cancel all the appointments for this afternoon."

"Then that explains the mob I passed on my way in a moment ago," Kim replied.

"I'm sorry." The nurse was watching her curiously, apparently trying to figure out what had brought Kim to the office so unexpectedly. "Can I make an appointment for another day? Dr. Stewart should be in tomorrow."

"That would be fine," Kim assured her quickly. She was eager to get away without being drawn into an awkward explanation.

"Is three o'clock good for you?"

"Perfect." Kim smiled and turned away. "See you then," she called back over her shoulder. But even as she did, Kim wondered if she was doing the right thing. What would she say to Dan? What did she want him to answer? Driving home, she was filled with doubts.

Every word that Valerie had poured out to her ran through Kim's mind. For the first time since Cliff ran out on her, Valerie was in love again. And Dan . . .? What did he feel? Unbearable as the thought was, Kim knew she at least had to face the possibility. Was she a closed chapter in Dan's life, and Valerie an exciting new story?

Chapter Eleven
At Dream's End

In the clear light of morning, Kim's doubts loomed even stronger. Thinking about whether or not to tell Dan as she tossed in her bed the previous night, thinking about it as she showered and brewed herself a pot of tea for breakfast, she kept asking herself what she would say when she was face to face with him.

I never forgot you, Dan. The amnesia was a curtain over my memories. But the instant it lifted I remembered everything about us. And I never stopped loving you, either. Even now, pregnant with John's baby, you are the one man in the world who owns my heart, just as surely as if you had locked it up and thrown away the key. I wanted to tell you months ago—before you went to South America—but I couldn't reach you. John kept me trapped in the house like a prisoner. The only way I could reach you was to leave a message on your answering machine. But you never answered it. I poured out my heart on that tape. And for all these disappointing, lonely months I believed you didn't care enough to answer me. Instead you never knew—never even suspected that every moment of the day and night I ache with love for you.

Once she'd made the speech in her own mind, though, Kim knew that she would never repeat it to Dan. Reluctantly, she went to the phone and dialed his number to cancel her appointment. Deep down Kim felt that she was canceling much more than an appointment, though. She felt as if she were wiping out the last ray of hope that she had secretly guarded. The future now loomed ahead of her like a black abyss.

Even anticipating the birth of her baby could not lighten the mood that fell over her. Dan would never be a part of her life again. Kim moved through the day on automatic pilot, overwhelmed by an unshakable sense of loss. It didn't help at all to tell herself that Dan had been out of her life for months. Because, true though it was, he had never been out of her heart. She had not fully accepted the fact that they would never be reunited. In her most glorious fantasy, the doorbell would ring and he would be standing on her step, a radiant smile lighting his handsome face, a message of eternal love shining from his midnight blue eyes.

"A fantasy and nothing more," Kim told herself aloud. Somehow she would have to find a way to go on with her life—without a dream to sustain her. Lost in thoughts about what was and would never be again, she heard a chime. At first it sounded like a distant bell, as if her memory were sending her a signal. Gradually, though, it became louder and more persistent, invading her daydreams and forcing her back to reality.

It took Kim several moments to realize that the chime was not echoing in her mind alone. Another unexpected visitor was ringing her bell. Rushing to the door, she flung it open and stared, stunned into silence. Dan stood on her front step. Just as in her dream, a radiant smile lit his handsome face and a message shone from his midnight-blue eyes—a message that seemed to speak of love.

"Hello, Kim," he said. His deep, warm voice sent shivers tingling the length of her spine. "It's good to see you."

She tried to find words to answer him, but her lips would only form a single word. "Dan!" she murmured, still unable to believe the vision in front of her was real.

"Aren't you going to ask me in?" he asked finally when she made no further move. "It's cold out here."

"I'm sorry," Kim managed to stammer. "It's just that . . . well, I was thinking about you," she admitted, "and here you are. It's been a long time since you came ringing my doorbell."

He nodded, seeming to search her face for a clue to what lay in her heart.

"Come on in." Kim turned away to hide her confusion. "I'll make you a cup of coffee or a drink—whatever you like." She knew she was talking too fast as she led the way into the living room, but she was too nervous to stop herself. Although she'd seen Dan from time to time since his return to Oakdale, it had only been in a crowd. Now here he was in her own house, his very presence turning her knees to jelly. She pinched her arm to convince herself it wasn't all her imagination. She was actually surprised when she felt a twinge of pain.

In spite of the December chill, Dan was wearing only a tweed sports coat. His single concession to the falling temperature was a navy-blue cashmere scarf, a shade deeper than his eyes. Taking it off, he tossed it over the arm of a club chair and sat down.

"I'll take that drink you were offering," he said with deceptive calmness. "A scotch on the rocks, if you've got it."

Kim was glad for the excuse to escape to the kitchen. Being alone with Dan even for a moment awakened tumultuous desires. Her cheeks flamed as if she'd been staring into a fire. Her heart pounded with excitement. Rattling bottles and ice trays to distract herself, she poured a whiskey for him and a glass of water for herself and carried them into the living room.

"You're the last person in the world I expected to find on my doorstep," she admitted as she served him.

"Disappointed?" Dan's inescapable eyes seemed to hold her a moment longer than they should if he was simply making a social call.

"How can you ask that?" she murmured, sitting across the room from him, well out of reach. It was the only safe place, she thought. An inch or two closer and she couldn't trust herself not to reach out and touch him.

Dan only shrugged in answer. "I was expecting to see you in the office this afternoon. When my nurse said you called and canceled, I decided to stop by to find out what you wanted to see me about," he explained.

"It wasn't anything—really," Kim insisted quickly. Susan's secret was filed away in her heart. The past was finished, the future was a chapter waiting to be written. If Dan still loved her, it would end "happily ever after." If his heart belonged to Valerie now . . . Kim couldn't bear to focus on the possibility, her sense of loss was so devastating.

"That's what I suspected." Dan was twirling the ice in his drink and smiling at her impersonally as if they had never been anything except the most casual of acquaintances. "I guessed you were worried about Betsy. She has a habit of dramatizing things in her own mind, and for a while there she was having a hard time accepting my relationship with Valerie. She built up a wall of resentment, but little by little Val's been chipping it down. Betsy has finally begun to accept her. It's made a big difference to both of them—and to Emily and me as well," he added.

Kim felt the hot bitter tears of loss fighting to be released. She wanted to weep—or scream —or fall at his feet and beg him to love her again and forever. Instead she forced herself to smile. Susan's secret was safely buried. Dan and Valerie . . . Valerie and Dan. Kim could never spoil someone else's chance for happiness just to satisfy her own needs. "I'm glad to hear that you're happy at last, Dan," she murmured. "This time I hope no one—and nothing—destroys it for you."

Searching Kim's eyes for a glimmer of the love that he'd cherished more than life itself, Dan saw only the reflection of her generous, caring spirit—not the deep, undying devotion that lay behind her words.

Hearing the doors open, Susan stepped into the hospital elevator, her attention absorbed in the stack of lab reports she'd received. She looked up just long enough to push the button for the sixth floor and, to her horror, found herself face to face with Dan. Instinctively, she tried to get off, but the doors snapped closed behind her and the elevator began its slow ascent.

Trapped! Susan thought with horror. Ever since revealing her secret to Kim, Susan had made a point of avoiding her ex-husband. She couldn't bring herself to face him again. What could he think of her now? How thoroughly he must despise her for interfering so cruelly in his life! Sure that Kim had told him all, Susan had gone out of her way to avoid bumping into Dan. She'd even canceled her weekly outings with Emily on the off chance that he would be home when she went to pick up her daughter.

But all her efforts were wasted. There was no escape from a moving elevator. The lab report she'd been studying shook in her hands, and her heart rate tripled. She felt fine beads of perspiration form on her brow.

"How are you, Susan?" Dan's resonant voice filled the elevator. "I thought you might be sick because you haven't been over to see Emily lately."

"I'm fine . . . never better," she answered nervously. Sneaking a quick glance up at him, she was amazed to find him smiling at her. He seemed genuinely pleased to see her.

Puzzled, she stared at him more boldly. "Are you sure you're okay?" she asked uncertainly.

"Of course, I'm sure," he laughed. "Why? Do I look bad or something?"

"No," she assured him. "I don't think you could look bad if you tried. I was just a little concerned, that's all," she hedged. "I thought maybe you had some . . . some bad news or something," she finished lamely.

"Bad news?" he echoed. "No, as a matter of fact, my life is running more smoothly than it has in years, thanks to Valerie."

"Valerie Conway?"

"The one and only." He grinned warmly. "I think she's good for me, and the girls are getting to like her better every day."

"What about Kim?" Susan blurted out in confusion.

A dark shadow swept over Dan's face, wiping out his smile. "What about her?" he said tightly.

"I was just wondering if you saw much of her," she answered nervously.

"I don't imagine Kim would have much time for me now that her baby is coming," he replied, "even if she did remember all that we once had." The elevator doors opened and Dan strode out.

Susan repeated his parting words over and over in her mind all the way home that night. *Even if she did remember . . . even if she did remember.* Dan's answer could only mean one thing: Kim had kept the secret of the erased tape.

"You're not going to believe this, Kevin. I still can't believe it myself," Susan blurted the moment she sat down at the table.

Laughing indulgently, Kevin leaned over to place a kiss on the tip of her nose. He'd invited her to meet him at the Barleycorn for dinner. One of their favorites, it was a small, informal restaurant specializing in steaks and chops broiled over an open hickory fire. Arriving early, he'd ordered sherry for him and club soda for her and sat down at their table to wait. "Calm down and tell me what it is that's so incredible."

"It's Dan," she said, taking a quick sip.

Kevin's face froze at the mention of her ex-husband. Even now, sure though he was of Susan's love, the very thought of Dan Stewart made him feel uneasy. Susan had been in love with Dan for so long that Kevin couldn't help feeling jealous. "What about him?" Kevin muttered.

Putting down her glass, Susan stared at him with eyes the size of platters. "Dan doesn't know," she told him. "I bumped into him in the hospital elevator, and it was absolutely clear. Kim hasn't breathed a word about the tape to him."

Kevin shrugged. "Well, you left it up to her, didn't you? Maybe she regrets making the tape. Or maybe her life has changed so much since then that she doesn't want to stir up the past. Kim has a right to make her own decision."

"But it's terrible," she wailed. "Here I was thinking I'd cleared my conscience and leveled with everyone. And instead I find out that I have to go on living with the same deceit. How do you think that makes me feel?"

Sipping his sherry slowly, Kevin studied her as closely as an artist about to paint her portrait—the small, sharp features offset by the huge dark eyes, the chestnut hair, the slender line of her throat. "I can't begin to imagine," he admitted finally. "How does it make you feel, Susan?"

"Guilty," she admitted. "I trusted Kim to tell Dan. Instead, he still thinks Kim's amnesia made her forget their whole relationship. I can't understand why she didn't rush right over to him. She's still in love with him—there's absolutely no question in my mind about that."

"Once she thought about it, maybe she decided it was better not to resurrect the past," Kevin suggested.

"But she's got no right to decide any such a thing," Susan insisted. "You said so yourself, Kevin. As long as Dan doesn't know, the whole embarrassing business can blow up in my face. What if Pat takes it into her head to spill the story to him? Have you thought of that?"

"Maybe you should have thought of it before you erased the tape," he pointed out sharply. "You did something unforgivable, Susan, and you've got to live with the consequences, one way or another."

Even as he answered, Susan was shaking her head. "I can't stand it. I don't know which is worse—Dan knowing or not knowing. Why doesn't she just tell him and get it over with? This way I have to keep wondering every time I see him: Does he know yet? Did Kim tell him today? It's like having the blade of a guillotine dangling over my head, twenty-four hours a day."

"Actually, when you think about it, Kim's decision isn't surprising at all," Kevin pointed out. Drumming the edge of the table thoughtfully with his fingertips, he said, "You have to remember the kind of woman Kim is. She thinks of everyone before herself—no matter how much she's hurting."

"But she wants Dan back. I just know she does," Susan insisted. "She as much as admitted it when I told her about the tape. It doesn't make any sense for her to keep silent. It's crazy, Kevin. Kim's just leaving the road open for Valerie to waltz right up to the altar with Dan."

The waiter came to take their dinner order, interrupting their conversation. But once they had made their selections, Kevin continued as if they'd never even paused.

While they were ordering, he'd watched Susan closely. The love between a man and woman was such a fragile mystery; ever present with it, like the flip side of a coin, was the fear of loss and betrayal. "Would that bother you so much?" he now asked quietly, holding her with the intensity of his gaze. "If there was a new Mrs. Stewart, I mean?"

Reaching across the table, Susan brushed his

cheek with her fingertips, her touch giving the answer his heart yearned to hear. "For a long, long time, I couldn't even bear to think of the possibility of Dan remarrying. But that was before you came into my life. Now I would wish him every happiness with his new wife."

Kevin smiled contentedly, satisfied that her answer came directly from her heart. "Maybe Kim feels the same way," he suggested thoughtfully.

"What do you mean?" Susan looked at him, puzzled. "There's no other man in her life now, unless you want to count Karl Strausfield, and I really don't think she's seriously involved with him."

"Neither do I," Kevin agreed. "In fact, Kim seems to me to be at one of the lowest points of her life. She's pregnant and alone—and very soon now she's going to discover how difficult it is to be a single parent. But no matter how tough her situation is, I can't imagine it making her bitter. The Kim Dixon I know is too warm and loving a person to step over anyone to help herself. Remember the reason why she didn't accept Dan's proposal in the first place? She didn't want you to be hurt. She was afraid that you'd start drinking again if she married Dan."

Susan nodded her head, understanding his logic. The guilt that she'd tried to eradicate with her confession washed over her again. "And now she's afraid of hurting Valerie?"

"Exactly." Kevin's face was a pattern of deep concern. "Kim is quite a woman. Now that Valerie has set her sights on Dan, Kim is willing to hold herself back rather than risk hurting either of them. I'm sure it's not only Valerie and Dan she's thinking of," he added. "Don't forget how fond Kim is of Betsy and Emily. It was just as tough for them as it was for Dan when Kim dropped out of their lives. Now that they're finally adjusting to Valerie, Kim is probably afraid of upsetting them again."

"Then, you think she's never going to tell Dan what happened?" Susan asked incredulously. "She's just going to sit by and watch Valerie steal the man she loves?"

"I don't think Kim will tell Dan your secret unless he stops seeing Valerie."

"But Valerie will never let him go," Susan protested.

"You're undoubtedly right," Kevin agreed. "And Kim probably knows that as well as, if not better than we do."

"That's terrible," she gasped.

"It's not terrible," Kevin corrected in his firm yet quiet way. "That's just the way Kim is. She's a very special person."

Susan lapsed into a tense silence. When their dinner was served, she ate mechanically, putting one bite in her mouth after the other but barely tasting a thing. Nothing was working out the way she'd planned.

Later that night, lying in bed alone, she

tossed uneasily. Kevin had wanted to stay, but she'd pleaded a headache for the first time since his love had entered her life.

"Let Kim make her own decision," Kevin had advised as he kissed her good-night at the door. But Susan couldn't accept his good counsel. Tossing and turning in her restlessness, she tried to invent the future, and every scenario left her mind in a turmoil. Through the crack in her bedroom curtain, she could just see the slice of a crescent moon. Usually the sight held her interest. But tonight it could as easily have been the light from a passing plane.

Although she loved Kevin with all her heart, nothing could ever change the fact that Dan was the first man in her life; the husband she'd pledged to hold fast, for better or worse; the father of her only child. Their lives would always be joined in one way or another. Dan could never be just a memory. Now that Kevin was filling her life with so much happiness, she was free to wish Dan nothing less. If she could give him the future she had destroyed for him, she would without hesitation.

Susan knew with absolute certitude that the love between Kim and Dan—the love she had shattered—had been true and deep. If she went to him now and made a full confession, would that love be rekindled? Would Dan be able to find the same happiness with Kim now that she was having John's baby?

The longer Susan tried to think, the more impossible her problem grew. What if she maintained her silence? Would Dan marry Valerie as a second choice? Or even worse, would someone else—someone like Pat Holland—whisper the bitter truth about the tape in Dan's ear? By the time the night sky lightened and the first violet-gray tinge of morning streaked the horizon, Susan had resolved her dilemma. Exhausted, she shut her eyes and whispered a solemn vow to herself as she slipped toward unconsciousness.

I, Susan Stewart, solemnly swear that I will stick to the decision I made tonight no matter what price I have to pay for it.

Chapter Twelve
The Hand of Fate

Sighing listlessly, Kim turned on the burner and set the small double-boiler of squash on the range top. Although she really didn't have much appetite, she forced herself to muster up some enthusiasm for the meal. She was spending another Saturday night alone. Karl had invited her to dinner, but she had begged off, saying she didn't feel up to socializing with her due date only a week away. But that wasn't the only reason she was staying home alone. She didn't want to inflict her company on anyone else. It would surely ruin anyone's evening, even the most sympathetic companion. Yearning for a familiar voice, she switched on the television and sank onto the couch.

Depression clung to Kim like a black shroud. It had begun with Susan's visit and deepened with Dan's. After that, even the weather seemed to be an enemy. The days had become remorselessly bleak. Storm warnings flashed on the news hourly, predicting a major blizzard with record-breaking snowfalls sweeping down from the Great Lakes. Kim didn't pay any attention. Any other pregnant woman would have been worried about how—and if—she would make it to the hospital. But Kim hadn't made any plans. She hadn't even asked a friend to stand by.

Ever since the masquerade party, John had telephoned daily to find out if her contractions had started. She was tempted to answer, "It's none of your business," but she always stopped herself, realizing how foolish she would have sounded. Much as she wished otherwise, the baby belonged to John as much as it did to her. Either she would have to learn to live with that fact or be prepared to fight continuous custody battles. She had learned long ago that John could be ruthless if he didn't get his way.

Occasionally, Kim consoled herself by thinking that the baby would change John for the better. But deep down she recognized the self-deception. After so many years of marriage, she knew John inside and out. She knew the obsessive love that seethed in his heart like a poison. There was absolutely no way he was going to leave her and the baby alone.

All through their marriage John refused to have children because he didn't want to share her—not even with a baby. Now that she had left him, he was determined to claim the child as his own, knowing that it was one way to gain access to Kim. Although John's motives were obvious, Kim couldn't find it in her heart to deny his paternal rights. Her fondest wishes, her deepest regrets, couldn't change the fact that the baby was John's, too.

Wandering into the kitchen, she turned the squash on low to simmer, then washed and prepared a Cornish game hen. While it was roasting, she arranged a tray for herself, complete with a linen placemat and napkin, a crystal water glass, and her best china. She had read somewhere that making a special dinner and creating a formal place setting, even if dining alone, could chase away the blues. But instead of putting her in a light mood, the single tray heightened her depression.

As they so often did, her thoughts turned to Dan. She wondered what he was doing that evening. Perhaps he and Valerie were preparing a meal, as well. Kim knew how much Dan enjoyed cooking, though she couldn't really picture Valerie with an apron on and a spatula in her hand.

Wondering if Betsy and Emily were helping them, Kim recalled an evening when she and Dan and the girls had prepared a dinner for his parents. Ellen and David Stewart had been celebrating their wedding anniversary, and the meal was to be a surprise for them. Dan's sisters, Annie and Dee, were there, as well as Ellen's grandfather, Judge Lowell.

Looking back on the evening now, Kim realized that her favorite part wasn't the delicious food or even the good company; she had loved the energetic and industrious spirit of the girls as they'd created the party's decorations. Betsy had made a seasonal centerpiece, and Emily had drawn cards for each place setting. Kim still had hers tucked away in her treasure box. She wondered if Valerie would have saved her place card, had she been there instead of Kim. Somehow, just as Kim couldn't picture her cooking, she couldn't imagine her as a doting, caring mother, either. Valerie just wasn't the domestic type.

The oven's timer rang shrilly, jarring Kim from her reverie. Listlessly she got up to rescue her hen before it became dry. As she turned off the oven, stabbing pain shot across her abdomen. It was so acute that she instinctively hugged herself and sat back down. Although the pain eased quickly, she was still shaken by its suddenness and intensity. Carefully, she started to stand up again. At her first step the pain returned with even greater severity.

Holding on to the furniture for support, she made her way into the bathroom very slowly. Just as she allowed herself a moment to catch her breath, a fresh stab of pain doubled her in two like a jackknife.

Dear God, don't let it be true, her mind screamed. *Not now*. Her head was so light that she had to clutch the towel rack to keep from falling over. *This can't be happening to me.*

She looked down and was shocked to see blood. *Something is wrong,* she thought in panic. *Something is seriously wrong!*

Leaning against the tiled wall, she breathed deeply to stop herself from fainting and tried to think clearly. "Call if the contractions are three minutes apart," the obstetrician had warned her. She turned her arm over to look at her watch and time herself. One . . . one and a half . . . two. Pain grabbed her so tightly she gasped in agony. The instant it quieted, she started timing again. Thirty seconds . . . sixty . . . ninety . . . one hundred. The contractions were coming stronger and faster—not even a full two minutes apart—and each pain was lasting longer.

"Telephone," she told herself aloud, her voice sounding foreign to her ears. "I have to telephone." But the phone was in the bedroom, and the distance from the bathroom loomed ahead like a ten-mile trek. Pulling herself up, she stood absolutely still for a moment until her head cleared. But she didn't dare let go of the towel rack. A frightening nightmare scenario whirled through her brain. *What if I can't make it to the phone?*

Beads of perspiration began to drip down her face and neck. She hesitantly inched toward the door into the hall. Her bedroom door

179

wasn't really far, but it may as well have been miles.

The passageway spun like the hall of a house of horrors. Even though Kim hugged the wall, she knew she'd never make it to the bedroom phone. "One step at a time," she murmured aloud to keep from panicking completely. "One step . . . one more." Glancing back, she realized that she'd made more progress than she thought. The bathroom was now two giant steps behind her . . . the bedroom probably three ahead.

Breathless, Kim rested against the wall to gather her waning strength for the next few inches. But the pain swept over her with a ferocity that made the previous contractions feel like the merest twinge by comparison.

"Please God, no!" she gasped, clutching her belly and doubling over helplessly. At that moment she couldn't think of the baby or the excitement of being a mother. She could only feel overwhelming agony. No one had prepared her for this. None of her friends had warned her how unbearable it would be.

Something must be wrong, she thought. *This pain can't be normal.*

The contractions were coming so fast and strong now they blocked out every feeling. The only thing she could focus on was how severe the next one would be. Could they keep on getting worse? It didn't seem possible, yet it took only seconds to show her that it was.

Folding her arms underneath her stomach and pressing tightly as if she could stem the pain that way, Kim staggered toward the bedroom. Just four more steps and she'd be there. Three . . . two. The white phone sat on the bedside table. She could see it through the open door. One call. One . . .

She rested against the doorjamb of her room to catch her breath between contractions. How foolish—yes, and arrogant—to think she could do everything alone. So many friends had offered to stay with her through the last month, had begged her to call them night or day, but she had refused to accept anyone's offer. The experience was too confused to allow anyone to share it with her—a truly bittersweet moment in her life. The thrill of having a baby at last was countered by the fact that it had been fathered by a man she didn't love. Poor John! Kim felt pity for him, and contempt, but also respect for his intelligence and skill as a physician. She felt many things, but not love . . . never love.

Measuring the gaping space from the door to the bed with a nervous glance, Kim forced herself to go the last mile. The pain was so wrenching, so enveloping that all she could see was blackness. She managed to lurch forward, hurling her body toward the bed. Her eyes were closed against the agony of the next contraction as her body bounced against the soft, satiny warmth of the comforter.

For a blissful second, she lay absolutely motionless, willing her body an instant of rest. Then, crawling up the bed, she reached out and grasped the cold plastic phone that seemed like a lifesaver. Her hands shaking, she dialed the number she had committed to memory.

"Doctor's office." A bored, impersonal voice answered on the third ring.

"Dr. Allen please," Kim said, relief overwhelming her. The doctor would get her to the hospital in time for the baby to be born. She wouldn't be alone any longer.

"Is this an emergency?" the voice questioned routinely.

"Yes, I'm in labor," Kim practically screamed into the receiver. "I have to talk to Dr. Allen right away."

"I'm sorry, ma'am. You've reached the doctor's answering service. If you give me your name and number, he'll get back to you."

"There's no time for that!" she cried.

"I'm sorry, that's the best I can do," the operator insisted. "Please give me your—"

"Kim Dixon, 555-9878," she burst out. "And please tell him to hurry."

Falling back on the pillow, Kim curled her legs against the fresh onslaught of pain. Labor could last for hours, she told herself. But the contractions were coming so fast and fiercely now, she knew that was just wishful thinking. *Please, God, keep my baby healthy*, she prayed.

Closing her eyes in pain, she felt herself slipping away. If she blacked out, she wouldn't hear the doctor's call. Pulling herself up on her elbow, she tried to sit up, but the effort was too exhausting.

With a low moan of defeat, she sank down again. The room spun like a carousel out of control. To hold on to consciousness, Kim tried to focus on a single item—the photograph of Betsy and Emily lying together in a huge mound of autumn leaves. But she kept losing the images. Her face contorted in a paroxysm of pain. Sweat bathed her face, and her clothes stuck to her like a second skin. She had to breathe in short, quick gasps until the contractions subsided, if only for a moment or two.

Time was running out. Kim felt her strength ebbing away. She hadn't eaten anything all day except a slice of melon at breakfast. The labor was so intense that she was growing too weak to fight any longer for her unborn baby or herself. The waves of pain seemed to be washing over her from a distant, distant shore. She felt detached, as if she were witnessing someone else suffering instead of experiencing it herself. She began drifting . . .

Suddenly a loud bell jangled in her brain, rousing her consciousness.

Instinctively she reached out and grasped the telephone.

"Kim, it's Dr. Allen," a calm, assured voice spoke in her ear.

Kim listened to the soothing voice and felt her body grow lax. She tried to find the strength to answer, but when she opened her mouth she couldn't remember what words to say.

"Kim!" The doctor's voice was strong and commanding, willing her back to consciousness. "Are you all right?"

"Coming . . . the baby . . ." she managed to whisper. "Baby . . ." Her eyelids drooped, her hand went limp, and the receiver dropped on the bed beside her.

Outside the delivery room door, Dr. Allen and John conversed in low, somber tones. The obstetrician was dressed in a hospital gown and hat, his mask hanging loose around his neck.

"I know you and Kim are separated," he was saying to John, "but I thought you would like to be notified. She should have someone with her." Dr. Allen knew that John had been barred from the hospital, but the welfare of his patient was his first concern.

"You did the right thing to call me," John replied. "I want to know exactly what happened."

Dr. Allen shook his head. "I wish I could tell you," he said, giving John's arm a reassuring squeeze. "All I can do is guess that she went into intense labor. By the time the ambulance reached her, she was unconscious."

"How is she now?" John's face was as white as the hospital walls.

"Still losing strength. It's a very difficult and prolonged labor." Dr. Allen's tone was as grave as his words. "I'm going to give her another fifteen or twenty minutes, only because I know how very much Kim wanted a natural child-birth. But even at that, I'm taking a calculated risk."

John nodded grimly. As a doctor, he knew all too well the perils Kim and their baby were facing.

The obstetrician continued speaking in a low, ominous voice. He relayed to John his findings of the preliminary examination he had done as soon as Kim had arrived in the ambulance. His words were not encouraging.

"You'll have to do a C-section." John wasn't questioning the other doctor; he was stating the inevitable.

"As I told you, John, I'm going to give Kim a few more minutes. It's a difficult decision, weighing what's best for both mother and child. If I'm wrong, it can mean not only infection but possible brain damage for the baby. As for Kim . . ." His voice trailed off. "I don't have to tell a physician like you."

John reached out and grabbed the other doctor's arm in an iron grip. "I'm going in there now, Allen, to see my wife. But get this clear: if it comes down to a decision of choosing either Kim or the baby, I want Kim saved."

The threat echoed unmistakably in John's voice, but Dr. Allen thought it was best to ignore it. Looking at John with the deepest sympathy, Dr. Allen shook his head. "I'm sorry, but I can't promise you that. I have to do what's right by my patient, and Kim made her decision months ago. She told me if there was any doubt at all, she wanted me to save the baby first. I hope it doesn't come to that, but—"

"There are no buts," John hissed. His face was twisted in a mask of anger and fear so that the veins on his neck stood out like ropes. "I'm giving the orders now, and I want my wife saved. If you're not going to do it, then I'll take over the case myself."

"You can't, John," the doctor reminded him calmly. "You're not even on the hospital staff anymore."

But John didn't stop to listen. Shoving the obstetrician aside, he pushed open the delivery room door and rushed in. At the foot of the delivery table, he stopped short and stared down at Kim's motionless body. Shock, horror, and agonizing fear clouded his features. Beyond her abdomen, which was stuck with electrodes to monitor the fetal heart rate, her face looked like a death mask. Her skin bore a grayish pallor, and her lips were drained of any color. Her eyes were closed, only the barest flutter of her lashes revealing that she was not comatose. Her short hair was damp and pushed off her face, accentuating the deathlike appearance.

With a sharp intake of breath, John steeled himself against the rush of bitter, angry tears that welled in his eyes as he looked at his wife. "Kim, darling. Kim," he called in a tender whisper. Walking around the side of the bed, he leaned over and stroked her moist forehead, smoothing the silky hair back from her temples. "Wake up, darling. Please, wake up," he urged in the same gentle voice.

Kim groaned as a spasm of pain shot through her. Glancing at the monitor attached to her right arm, John saw that the meter measuring the severity of her contractions had moved only a few degrees. Her labor had quieted to almost a standstill.

Outside the door, Dr. Allen waited nervously. He was giving Dixon a minute alone with his wife—a minute he prayed she and the baby could spare—then he was going in to take control.

"Can you hear me, darling?" John was pleading, his voice like a whispered prayer.

Slowly, very slowly, Kim's eyelids opened and she looked up at him. Her eyes, glazed and unseeing, pictured what was in her dreams.

187

Through the miasma of pain, the smallest smile formed on her white lips, and they moved—dryly, inaudibly at first, then with a word, a sound too soft to catch.

"Do you recognize me, Kim?" John asked, his voice begging her to wake up, to snap out of the delirium that made her dazed and lost to him. "Do you know who I am?"

The little smile flickered on her lips again. "You came," she murmured happily, reaching out to him, as if her hand were drawn to his by an irresistible magnetic force. "I knew you'd come," she murmured dreamily again.

Her eyes closed slowly as if the effort of holding them open had become too much for her. But the dreamlike image stayed before her: dark curly hair framing a ruggedly handsome face, midnight-blue eyes shining like her highest hopes, a deeply cleft chin, a radiant smile erasing all the broken promises and misdirected cues. In her weakness and pain, she imagined Dan, not John, was leaning over her bedside.

"I love you . . . I always loved you," she whispered, revealing the secret she'd guarded so long in her heart. "I will always love you."

"I love you, too, darling. You know I do." John's voice trembled with unexpected joy. Finally in her weakest, most critical moment, Kim was admitting to what he longed to hear for so many years.

She squeezed his hand, believing that Dan had finally come back to her. "And you'll love my baby?" She strained to get the words out. "Promise me you'll try."

An elated laugh escaped from John's lips. "I won't have to try, Kim. I love the baby already because it's yours . . . ours."

"Ours . . ." She repeated the magical word over and over in her mind. "Our baby." Even though he wasn't the father, Dan would love the baby as if it were his own, Kim thought, and so would Betsy and Emily. At last they'd all be a family . . . a perfect family. Although her eyes were closed and her lips quiet, her fingers tightened around his in an unmistakable signal of love.

Kim loved him and wanted him, John thought excitedly. Motherhood had broken down the barriers that had kept them apart. *You and me and baby makes three.* . . . Feeling the heightened pressure of her fingers, John leaned down and kissed her forehead. It seemed too good to be true, and yet it was. Kim was his again—and he would never let her go.

A Very Special Offer for Our Readers

THINK•ABOUT PICTURE ACTIVITY CARDS

Now, you can give your preschooler, kindergartener, or first grader a head start in developing his or her *thinking skills*— thinking skills that will affect your child's learning abilities throughout the early and later school years—in fact, throughout life.

THINK•ABOUT PICTURE ACTIVITY CARDS are now available to parents, for the very first time.

These are the very same cards used by thousands of teachers in nursery schools and elementary schools throughout the country—the same cards that were the main selection of the Early Learning Book Club and the Library of Special Education.

THINK•ABOUT PICTURE ACTIVITY CARDS are a fun-filled, imaginative way to teach children how to solve problems. The back of each card has clear directions for each learning activity. *The program requires absolutely no special training on the part of the parent.* Each card is cheerfully illustrated with an everyday place, person, or thing that involves your child in problem solving and reasoning skills.

THINK•ABOUT PICTURE ACTIVITY CARDS sell to schools for $19.95, but now you can receive them for just $12.95 plus $2.75 for shipping and handling (a savings of $7.00 from the school price).

The cards are in 2 colors on glossy, heavy, durable stock, shrink-wrapped to keep them clean, and they come with a kraft envelope in which your child can store them. Thirty-six of the cards are a large 8x10, and sixty are an easy-to-handle, 5x8 size. The program is published by Center for Media Development, Inc., publishers of early learning and primary grades teaching material.

For your set of THINK•ABOUT PICTURE ACTIVITY CARDS, send a check or money order for $15.70 ($12.95 plus $2.75 for shipping). If you wish to purchase 2 sets, the total cost is $27.50 (a savings of an additional $3.90). Make checks or money orders payable to: Center for Media Development, Inc. Dept. G, Box 51, Great Neck, N.Y. 11021. Thank you.

Name _____

Address _____

City _____ State _____ Zip Code _____

THINK•ABOUT PICTURE ACTIVITY CARDS—
a great start for your child!

Soaps & Serials ®

Only from Pioneer Communications Network, Inc.

OVER 9 MILLION BOOKS IN PRINT!